NORTH OF THE BORDER

NORTH OF THE BORDER

by
Ben Bridges

MAGNA PRINT BOOKS
Long Preston, North Yorkshire,
England.

British Library Cataloguing in Publication Data.

Bridges, Ben, *1958—*
    North of the border.

    ISBN 0-7505-0185-5

First Published in Great Britain by Robert Hale Ltd., 1990

Published in Large Print 1991 by arrangement with Robert Hale
Ltd., London

Printed and bound in Great Britain by
Redwood Press Limited, Melksham, Wiltshire.

For Colin Clynes

ONE

Some men take forever to die.

Deputy U.S Marshall Padraig O'Hare did.

He lay on his back, staring up at the wide Montana sky, and died slowly, by degrees, with most of his stomach splashed across the grass beneath him.

O'Hare was a big red-headed Irishman who had spent most of his life keeping the peace behind one tin star or another. His final case had involved four trappers who raped and killed a woman in Choteau. O'Hare had tracked them up into the Lewis Range, a hundred or so miles to the northwest, then cornered them not far from the Hungry Horse Reservation.

They'd made a fight of it, of course. But O'Hare had expected they would. And being a better than fair shot, he'd plugged two of the sumbitches before they could even clear leather.

The third man, however, had been faster.

And so had the fourth.

When O'Hare's fellow marshals found him a week or so later, the rapists' deathly-quiet

9

campsite told its own grim story. Around the cold black smudge of the stone-ringed fire, all four trappers lay stiff as boards, sprawled in various attitudes of sudden, violent death. About ten feet away, O'Hare too, lay sleeping his final sleep. He had a .45 calibre bullet in his right leg, just above the kneecap, and his guts had literally been shredded by two barrels of .00 buckshot from the sawn-down Purdey one of the rapists still clutched in his bloodless claws.

O'Hare had died slow and hard; the expression on his face spoke eloquently of his suffering. But at least the Irishman had checked out knowing that he had taken his killers with him.

That was probably why the men who found his body read the twist of his lips in two ways; as either one last, agonised grimace—or the faint but satisfied smile one usually reserves for a job well done.

Carter O'Brien hadn't really known the lawman all that well. Fate had thrown them together a couple of times, back when O'Brien had been a Pinkerton detective, and they'd gotten along well enough. But O'Hare had never been more than a passing acquaintance, and the feeling, he knew, was mutual.

Still, he could hardly refuse to attend

O'Hare's wake and funeral when the wire from the Irishman's widowed mother finally caught up with him—especially since he was only about a hundred miles away, in Great Falls, Montana.

Reluctantly, then, he forgot all about living it up with the thousand dollars General George Crook himself had paid him to ride shotgun on the beautiful wife of a renegade Apache warrior*, and saddling up his most recent acquisition, a 1200-lb quarter-horse that stood fifteen hands at the shoulder, he set out for Missoula.

O'Brien was a tall, compact man whose lean, lived-in face had been burned the colour of copper by more than thirty-five summers. His pale blue eyes, too, had seen more life and death in those years than many a man twice his age, because being an incurable drifter with a weakness for adventure, O'Brien had tried his hand at just about everything from nursing cows and bouncing drunks to prizefighting, bounty hunting and scouting for the Army.

In '68 he'd pinned on the badge of town marshal in Garfield, Texas. In '71 he joined Pinkerton's National Detective Agency. Since late '72, however, he'd been making his living as a professional soldier of fortune, an occupation

* As told in *SQUAW MAN*

for which he was ideally suited. After all, the Colt Lightning at his right hip and the virtually-priceless Winchester 'One In One Thousand' in the scabbard on his scratched Texas double-rig weren't just for show.

There was no need for iron at Padraig O'Hare's funeral, however. O'Brien and about fifty other mourners—most of them representatives from one law-enforcement agency or another—stood in respectful silence as the Irishman was planted. Then, once the ceremony was concluded and O'Hare's mother led away sobbing, everyone repaired to the nearest saloon for a little liquid comfort, leaving the bone-orchard in small groups of three or four.

'You knew O'Hare well?' asked a tall, grey-headed man with a handlebar moustache of the same colour. O'Brien had noticed him the night before, at the wake. He was about O'Brien's height, six feet two, with an equally trail-worn face and flinty grey eyes. He looked about forty-some years of age, and was dressed in a black broadcloth jacket, plain white shirt and sage-grey whipcord pants. In his long-fingered hands he held a dusty old campaign hat that had seen better days, and nestled in his right-hand holster was a very business-like .38 calibre New Line Police Colt.

'Not well, no,' O'Brien replied honestly.

'We rode the same trail a time or two, but that was all.'

The grey-eyed man fingered his moustache thoughtfully as he turned his attention to the elderly grave-digger who was now beginning to shovel dirt back into the hole. They were the only ones left in the green, sunshine-filled cemetery now, they and about four thousand busy insects flying in seemingly aimless patterns around a veritable forest of headstones and plain wooden markers. The sepulchre-like silence was broken only by birdsong, and Missoula's clamour had no place there.

'*I* knew him well,' the other man muttered quietly. 'When we both worked out of the Tucson office. He was an all-right feller, was O'Hare. Fair, honest and dedicated.'

O'Brien indicated the shield pinned to the man's lapel. 'You're a U.S marshal,' he remarked.

'Kind of,' said the other man.

O'Brien found the reply curious. 'What does that mean?' he asked bluntly.

The U.S marshal smiled. 'If you could see my deputies,' he replied, 'you wouldn't need to ask.' Extending his right hand, he said, 'The name's Frost, by the way. Abel Frost. Pleased to know you.'

As they shook, O'Brien introduced himself.

13

He still couldn't puzzle out exactly who Frost might be, and never in a decade would he guess that the tall man actually headed-up up a six-man crew of Government-backed trouble-busters known collectively as 'The Wilde Boys'—law-enforcers who were, in reality, all convicted criminals themselves.

'Come on, O'Brien,' Frost said, cutting in on his thoughts. 'I'll buy you a drink.'

They turned and started back towards the dusty grey bulk of Missoula, rising like a faded tintype about three hundred yards to the north. At the cemetery gates, however, two men stood watching them with undisguised interest.

'Friends o'yours?' Frost enquired casually.

O'Brien examined them from beneath the shade of his curl-brimmed, tobacco-brown Stetson. 'Nope.'

The first man was of medium height, stocky, ruddy-faced and athletic-looking even though his conservative grey suit marked him as some sort of pen-pusher. He was around five years O'Brien's junior, with curly black hair cut short, a square, dimple-pitted jaw and pleasant, well-proportioned features that made him look not unlike a back-East college sophomore.

His coloured sidekick was obviously hired muscle. Taller, thinner and older by maybe as

14

much as twenty years, he was dressed in a plain grey shirt and California pants tucked into spurless stovepipe boots. A shin-length off-white duster covered most of his spare frame, but he looked like the kind of feller who could handle himself, and unlike the younger white man, he wore a formidable weapons-belt and a shell-filled bandolier across his narrow chest.

When no more than sixty feet separated them, the white man, who had been rubbing the tip of his right high-button shoe against the back of his left pants'-leg in an effort to shine it, stepped into their path.

'Excuse me,' he said amiably enough. 'Which of you gentlemen might be Mr Carter O'Brien?'

O'Brien and Frost slowed down, Frost keeping a watchful eye on the black man still standing beneath the shade of some rust-and golden-leafed aspens that formed a natural wall around the cemetery.

'I *might* be,' O'Brien replied, reaching up to touch the brim of his hat with his left hand. 'It kind of depends on who wants to know.'

The genial smile that spread across the other man's ruddy face revealed teeth that were both even and well-kept. 'Forgive me,' he said, coming forward to offer his right hand. 'Allow me to introduce myself. I am Roddy Bruce-Morgan, late of the Hudson's Bay Company

15

up in Yukon Territory.'

'Yukon Territory?' O'Brien echoed, eyeing the smaller man with renewed interest. 'That's up in Canada, isn't it?'

'It is indeed, sir.'

O'Brien said, 'You're quite a way off your usual stamping-grounds then, aren't you?'

Bruce-Morgan chuckled. 'Only temporarily, I assure you.' He turned his easy-going brown eyes Frost's way. 'I'm sorry to have intruded upon you during your hour of mourning,' he said, addressing them both formally in a gentle, 'r'-rolling Scottish accent. 'Unfortunately my schedule does not permit me a more leisurely approach.'

'Approach?' said O'Brien.

Roddy Bruce-Morgan met his quizzical gaze levelly. 'I am here to offer you a business proposition,' he replied, dropping his voice a touch. 'Assuming you're not already engaged elsewhere, of course.'

'I'm not,' O'Brien confessed. Guessing he had nothing to lose by hearing the smaller man out, he said, 'All right, Morgan—I'm listening.'

The scotsman glanced awkwardly up at Frost, and taking the hint, Frost said, 'I figure I'll go on ahead while you fellers talk. Maybe 'I'll see you later, O'Brien.'

O'Brien turned to him and they shook again. 'Maybe you will, Frost. So long.'

The tall marshal tipped his hat to Bruce-Morgan, threw another wary glance at the black man in the shade, then strode off through the gates and up the rutted track that led back to town.

O'Brien, watching him go, swept off his Stetson to run his left hand through his close-cropped salt-and-pepper hair. He was a handsome man in an odd kind of weather-beaten way, and his ears were cauliflowered from his earlier days as a pugilist.

As he set the hat back atop his head, Roddy Bruce-Morgan called the black man over and made introductions. 'This is Chester Kane, a valued colleague in this grand venture.'

O'Brien and the negro shook hands. Kane had a dark, unsmiling face with flared nostrils, thick lips and some snow up around his temples. His dark eyes gave nothing away as they traded stares; their whites, O'Brien noted, were actually the palest yellow.

'And what "grand venture" might that be?' O'Brien enquired, addressing Bruce-Morgan.

The Scotsman glanced around the graveyard either checking to make sure they were alone or looking for a place where they might take the weight off. Finally he spotted a likely-

17

looking spot under some more aspens thirty yards away, where a hard plank bench had been erected, and indicated that they head towards it.

'First things first,' he said affably as they started walking. 'I daresay you're wondering how I managed to find you in this somewhat prodigious land, and why I know without any shadow of a doubt that I can trust you to keep whatever I'm about to tell you to yourself.'

'It had crossed my mind,' O'Brien responded drily. They reached the shaded grass verge and sat down. Kane, however, remained standing, his eyes watchful and his manner alert.

'You've come highly recommended to me, Mr O'Brien,' Bruce-Morgan confessed. 'Our mutual friend, Senator Aaron Norris of Pittsburgh, Pennsylvania, speaks highly of you indeed. When first I confided my plans to him and told him the kind of man I was looking for, he put your name forward without hesitation.'

O'Brien grunted. He remembered Aaron Norris well. He'd gone south of the border to bust the senator out of a Mexican jail about two years before*. If he and Bruce-Morgan were

* As told in *MEXICO BREAKOUT*

as friendly as Bruce-Morgan implied, then O'Brien guessed he, like the late O'Hare, must be an all-right feller.

'Finding you was a simple enough matter,' the Scotsman continued. 'Aaron told me that you based yourself in Tombstone, Arizona. When I wired you there, your landlady replied that you were in Great Falls. In Great Falls the Western Union office replied to say that any message I might care to send would be forwarded to you here, in Missoula.'

'Well, you found me all right,' said O'Brien. 'And a right smart job you made of it. But suppose we get down to cases now?'

'Certainly, sir, certainly.' Bruce-Morgan sobered and leaned forward in the manner of a conspirator. 'I'll say it plain, Mr O'Brien. I have a proposition to put to you that is absolutely certain to make everyone involved very wealthy. That said, however, I feel I ought to warn you that it is not without risks. They are a rough breed of men up in Alaska, sir. Life grows cheap if one man's death means another may survive.'

'Hang fire a minute, Morgan,' O'Brien cut in. 'I think you're rushing ahead of yourself just a tad. What's all this about Alaska?'

The Scotsman looked at him in puzzlement. He was so fired-up by the thought of his 'grand

19

venture' that he had assumed for a moment that O'Brien was already privy to his plans.

'Alaska is our eventual destination,' he explained confidentially. 'To be precise, sir, the very *heart* of the Alaskan goldfields.'

O'Brien couldn't keep the smile off his lips. 'So that's it,' he said without criticism. 'You aim to join all those other colour-hungry sourdoughs up there and make your fortune panning for gold.'

'Oh no,' Bruce-Morgan replied with a shake of the head. 'Quite the contrary, Mr O'Brien. I plan to take a commodity far more valuable than that *into* Alaska, and once there, sell it for top dollar.'

Again O'Brien felt a renewed stirring of interest. 'A commodity...? What the hell kind of commodity could be more valuable than gold?' he asked.

It was Chester Kane who supplied the answer. Taking his eyes off their quiet, headstone-littered surroundings, he said in a low voice, 'Food.'

'To be precise, sir,' Bruce-Morgan went on, 'two Conestoga wagons filled with all manner of foodstuffs. Airtights, dried fruits, flour, sweetening and so on. Tobacco, baker's chocolate, home comforts of that type. And one hundred and fifty prime Hereford cows. Mr O'Brien—virtually two hundred thousand pounds of meat on the hoof!'

Sitting there on the hard plank bench, O'Brien began to get the feeling that he was missing the point. How were a couple of over-stuffed supply wagons and a hundred-fifty head of cattle going to make them all rich? Unless—

'Haven't they got any food of their own up north, Morgan?' he asked lightly.

Chuckling, the Scotsman shook his head. 'No, sir! At least, not in the way that you or I might view it. And that's the beauty of the whole scheme!'

But O'Brien still couldn't grasp it. 'Maybe you'd better explain it some more,' he said.

Bruce-Morgan nodded equably. 'Of course.'

Ever since America had bought Alaska from the Russians in 1867, a steady stream of veteran prospectors from California, Colorado, Montana and British Columbia had been drawn north of the border by the promise of gold. Although gold-strikes of any real consequence had yet to materialise, however, the diggers remained optimistic.

'There's been just enough colour taken out of the land around Juneau and the upper Yukon basin to convince both the sourdoughs and cheechakos—tenderfoots, you'd call them in these parts—that a big strike is just around the corner,' Bruce-Morgan went on. 'Why, some of them are already sluicing twenty, twenty-five dollars'-worth of gold out of their claims every day as it is.'

'But?' O'Brien prompted.

'But,' the Scotsman replied, 'the land is against them, sir. It's not about to give up its riches without a struggle.

'Alaska,' he went on, 'encompasses about half a million square miles, of which one hundred and seventy thousand at least are constantly covered in ice. At the moment, the prospectors working the fields in the interior are still enjoying reasonable, if damp, weather conditions.

'But a few weeks from now, winter will set in. Night-time temperatures will drop to sixty below, and the days won't be much better. The rivers will ice up and all water traffic will cease. Overland trails, too—precarious and inhospitable at the best of times—will be lost beneath snow—drifts fifteen, thirty feet deep.

'To all intents and purposes, Mr O'Brien, all those sourdoughs will find themselves entirely cut off from the outside world. And unless they've had the foresight to get in enough supplies to see them through till next March or April—which I very much doubt—

22

they'll starve. If you don't believe me, just take a look at previous winters, when hungry prospectors have been known to eat moose-meat usually reserved for their dog-teams,' Bruce-Morgan went on grimly. 'To eat reindeer too, and eventually the dogs themselves.'

'They even been known to eat each *other* when things is *real* bad,' Kane murmured ghoulishly.

'I can see why your supplies'll be worth their weight in gold, then,' O'Brien allowed. 'Providing you can get them through, that is.'

'Exactly,' agreed the Scotsman. 'And that is where you come in, O'Brien. Ahead of us we face a journey of not less than twelve hundred miles. At least once, when we reach Alaska and word of our enterprise gets out, we are bound to encounter brigands who would take our merchandise away from us.'

'And you want me to make sure they don't get away with it.'

'To handle the security, yes.' Bruce-Morgan nodded. 'At the moment my sister and I have seven men on our payroll—a driver for each of the wagons, four cowboys to handle the Herefords, and Chester here, who will also be riding shotgun on the entire expedition.

'Chester is a good man, Mr O'Brien,' the Scotsman said proudly. 'One of the best. He's

23

just finished a fifteen-year hitch in the Army and served honourably as a First Sergeant in the U.S Coloured Infantry during your Civil War. But he's only one man, sir, and to be perfectly honest with you, this trip carries more than enough responsibility for two.'

O'Brien considered everything he'd heard so far. 'You're sure this "enterprise" of yours can't go wrong?' he asked.

'Absolutely.'

'And you've got your route all mapped out?'

'Of course. Our wagons and cattle are presently encamped just outside of Seattle. It is my intention to charter a schooner there, sail north as far as Yakutat, then travel inland to the goldfields around Forty Mile by a combination of wagon and sledge. It will be a slow-moving trek, I know—but one not without its rewards.'

'What about your sister? I take it she'll be staying in Seattle?'

'Ginny?' Bruce-Morgan replied. 'My goodness, sir, no! She'll be coming with us—and just you try to stop her!' He chuckled again, as if he weren't just about to embark upon a journey laced liberally with danger at all, then turned serious again. 'Anyway, Mr O'Brien, both Ginny—Imogen, that is—and I have sunk all the funds at our disposal into this affair, and being a canny lass in matters of business, she's determined to see that our investment does indeed reach its destination.'

The blue-eyed fighting man sighed thoughtfully. He didn't like the idea of having a woman along, although he knew from personal experience that they were usually tougher and more resilient than men gave them credit for. 'How much are you offering me to say yes to this, Morgan?' he asked speculatively.

Bruce-Morgan's brown eyes glittered. 'Two thousand dollars,' he replied with a flourish.

O'Brien met his stare and said, 'I'll do it—for *five*.'

The Scotsman's mouth fell open. '*What?* Really, Mr—'

'Two thousand dollars is hardly much more than a dollar-fifty a mile,' O'Brien pointed out. 'And if all goes well, your cargo alone should net you well in excess of three hundred thousand, so don't tell me you can't afford it.'

The Scotsman's ruddy face crimsoned up even more as he switched his gaze away to the bird-filled garden of death before them. O'Brien could almost see his lips moving as he mentally revised his calculations. Chester Kane must have seen it too, because he came nearer and said with a rare smile, 'Don't forget to times that five thousand by two.'

Roddy Bruce-Morgan turned back to both of them. 'Four thousand five hundred *each*,' he said stiffly. 'And *possibly* a bonus of one thousand dollars to be split equally between you at trail's-end.'

O'Brien glanced up at the black man. 'What do you think?' he asked, more to win Kane over to his side than anything else; after all, the job would be easier if they acted as a team instead of two independent spirits.

'It'll do,' Kane replied shortly.

O'Brien climbed to his feet, the prospect of the coming adventure making a smile rise easily to his lips. 'Put it there, Morgan,' he said, sticking out his right hand. 'You got yourself a deal.'

It turned out that Bruce-Morgan and Kane had only rolled into Missoula about an hour before. In their desire to locate O'Brien they hadn't even bothered to find themselves lodgings. They'd just left their travel-gear down at the railroad station and set about asking around until they found out about O'Hare's funeral, and the fact that O'Brien would be attending it.

'To be honest,' Bruce-Morgan said as the three of them worked their way back to the cemetery gates, 'it wasn't worth looking for board anywhere. We can't afford to tarry overlong in Missoula, you see. That schedule I spoke of earlier—it's pretty tight, Mr O'Brien, and getting tighter all the while if we're still to find a boat willing to sail north this close to winter.'

'I understand,' O'Brien replied. 'And I'll be ready to move out again just as soon as I've collected my gear from my hotel room. Are there any more trains going west from here today, do you know?'

'They's a Northern Pacific bound for Tacoma leavin' at one,' Kane replied softly, his accent betraying his deep-South upbringing. 'We can gets a stagecoach from they up to Seattle, arrive 'bout six, seven o'clock tomorrow night.'

'Right.'

The time already being somewhere around noon, they arranged to meet up again at the railroad depot in thirty minutes, at which time Bruce-Morgan would be able to hand over a bank draft for one half of O'Brien's salary and then arrange passage for them all aboard the next train west.

When they split up, O'Brien headed back to his lodgings. Around him, Missoula's streets were stirring with a somewhat sluggish flow of mid-day traffic, but although the boardwalks were fairly busy, he saw no sign of Abel Frost.

Dust stirred up by the passing of wagons and horses rose slowly in sunlit, butter-coloured clouds. Here he saw brawny miners, there a few *chaparrera*-clad cowboys heading for the saloon. At last his hotel loomed large, a three-storied clapboard structure with an elegant false-front that added the appearance of one more floor, and he swung right, collected his key from the short, sixtyish desk-clerk and went on up to his second-floor room.

He hadn't been in there much more than five minutes before a light rapping at the door made him turn around. Wondering who in hell it could be (for he was largely unknown this far north), he crossed the carpet to answer it.

Two men stood in the dim corridor outside, a smooth-smiling city slicker-type dressed in a black hammertail coat over smart grey pants and spats, and a shorter, meaner-looking side-winder with the build of a pit bull and the face of a pretty unsuccessful prizefighter. Again he categorised them as pen-pusher and hired muscle, in that order.

'Mr O'Brien?' the city slicker-type ask-ed, oozing a wider, more confident smile. He offered his soft right hand for shaking. 'The name is Goodlight,' he said, as if that should mean something. 'Harvey Goodlight. And this is my, ah, foreman, J P Riley. May we come in?'

O'Brien paused, disliking and distrusting the pair of them on sight. 'I'm kind of busy right now,' he replied brusquely.

'This won't take but a minute,' Goodlight said pleasantly. 'And it concerns our mutual acquaintance, Mr Bruce-Morgan.' He caught the flash of suprise in O'Brien's bleached blue eyes and smiled wider. 'May I? Thanks.'

He and Riley stepped into the room and O'Brien closed the door behind them, then turned to face them. Goodlight was fifty or thereabouts, his face long and jowly, his eyes green and shifty, his smile just left of centre and broad enough to reveal long but orderly teeth. He took off his grey muley hat, showing black hair macassared flat to his head, and came to a halt over by the window, so that the sunshine spilling through the patterned lace of the curtain threw grey blotches over his head and shoulders.

J P Riley, by contrast, kept his sandy Plainsman's hat on. He was about O'Brien's age, mid-thirties, around five feet seven, heavy-chested and standing on legs as bowed as boiled frankfurters. He had a dark, square face with heavy black brows and a ferrety, broken nose that seemed, at one time, to have wandered across his face and wound up stuck fast just under his right eye. He had black eyes, O'Brien noticed, cruel as a sandstorm, and a cold, faintly mocking smile. He also had a habit of humming under his breath. He wore a dark-blue shirt and black pants, and carried a .44 calibre Remington Army model Number 3 in the cutaway holster he wore tied down to his left hip.

'Packing for the trek to Alaska?' Goodlight remarked easily, indicating the saddle-bags, war-bag and Winchester on the sagging bed.

'Alaska?' O'Brien echoed, deciding to play dumb.

But Goodlight saw through him at once. 'Oh, come on now, let's not be cagey. Cards on the table, huh?' When O'Brien made no response, something died in Goodlight's eyes; to be precise, whatever it was that gave them the illusion of warmth. 'All right,' he said. 'I'll go first.

'Roddy intends to go ahead with this scheme of his to run grub up to Seward's Folly, right?' he said, using the less than complimentary handle for Alaska which had been coined after Secretary of State William H Seward had bought the Great Land without really knowing what to do with it. 'And he's hired you to make sure it gets there intact.'

'Has he?' O'Brien asked blandly.

Goodlight's chest swelled for a second or so as he prepared himself for a sharp retort. Then he cooled down a little and took a gold watch out of his grey vest pocket to find out the time.

'How much is he paying you, O'Brien?' he asked. 'A couple of thousand? Three? Whatever it is, I'll *double* it.'

O'Brien eyed him with a poker face. 'That's mighty generous,' he allowed. 'But I get the feeling that you'd want me to do something almighty sneaky in return for all that money.'

Much to his suprise Goodlight said, 'Yes, I would. I'd want you to finger the location of his wagons and cattle for me, and when the time is right, help me take the whole shebang over, lock, stock and barrel.'

Well, O'Brien told himself, *he's direct if nothing else.*

With genuine curiosity he asked, 'Just who the hell *are* you, Goodlight?'

'A man like any other,' Goodlight replied smoothly, 'who wants to get rich in a hurry.'

Smiling without noticeable humour, O'Brien said, 'I think you'd better get out of here, the pair of you.'

But Goodlight held his ground. 'Didn't you hear me? I said I'd double whatever that damn-

31

fool Scotsman's paying you. That's fair, isn't it? I mean, since when did hired guns get picky about who pays their wages?'

O'Brien reached for the door handle with his left hand. 'I won't tell you again,' he warned ominously. 'Now get out.'

Goodlight's shoulders sagged and he looked supremely disappointed by O'Brien's refusal to do business with him. He said, 'Ten thousand dollars, tops. And that's my absolute limit, in case you're hoping to push the price any higher.'

'The only place I aim to push the price,' O'Brien said in a low voice, 'is up your ass if you don't get out of here inside the next thirty seconds.'

J P Riley stopped humming and it got very quiet in the room. O'Brien switched his gaze to the hired man and saw by the look in his black eyes that he was weighing up the pros and cons of hauling iron. Immediately he spread his own legs wider, for better balance if it should come to shooting.

Then Harvey Goodlight reached up to plant his muley hat atop his macassared black hair and said sharply, 'All right, O'Brien. Have it your own way. But the next time we meet, you might be sorry that we never got around to joining forces.' He glanced at Riley. 'Come

32

along, J P—we've got places to go.'

O'Brien opened the door and watched them leave, then kicked it shut and got on with his packing.

TWO

Fifteen minutes later O'Brien went back downstairs, threw two quarters on the counter and asked the desk-clerk to find a boy to take his gear down to the livery on Murphy Street and have the stable-lad get his horse ready for riding. While the desk-clerk said yes sir, he'd get right onto it, O'Brien turned his head to look out through one of the double doors and across the street.

A log-built store met his gaze, its dusty, smeared windows reflecting the hotel. To the left of the store stood a millinery, to the right a club-room above which according to a weathered shingle, sat the premises of a dentist which could be reached by a narrow side alley.

O'Brien scanned the windows of each building for any sign that might confirm that Goodlight had set someone to watch him, but they mirrored only his own side of the street.

'You're leavin' us then, Mr O'Brien?' asked the clerk.

O'Brien turned back to him. 'Huh? Oh— yeah.'

34

'You'll be wantin' to settle your bill, then?'

'If you've got the figure handy.'

The desk-clerk did. He named it and O'Brien peeled some bills from his bank-roll. Then he retraced his steps upstairs and closed his room-door behind him.

Edging over to the window, he peered cautiously through the lace. The street was busier now than it had been. The sun, now past its zenith, threw shadow over half its length. But although O'Brien's inspection was painstaking, he spotted no-one loitering suspiciously on any corner. Furthermore, the steady flow of customers in and out of the stores along the other side of the street told him that no potential assassin was using any of them for cover.

But that dentist's surgery... that was something else again...

Maybe he was being over-cautious. Hell, after the kind of life he'd led, he didn't know how to behave anyway else. But this time he felt that his precautions were valid. There was a lot of money at stake in Bruce-Morgan's plan, and now that Harvey Goodlight knew exactly where O'Brien's loyalties lay, he wouldn't want him trotting off to forewarn the Scotsman of his plans for a takeover.

He might just decide to silence O'Brien before O'Brien could make it down to the railroad depot, then.

He gnawed thoughtfully on his lower lip, blue eyes narrowed in concentration as he focused on the dentist's window. A minute later he'd settled on a course of action, and making sure that his gear lay ready for collection, he quit the hotel room, cat-footing as far as the large casement window at the end of the corridor.

As he'd suspected, it opened out onto a rickety set of fire stairs that cut a zigzag course down to the backyard. Making sure that no-one was lurking down *there*, he hauled up the window and let himself out, then descended to the cobbled yard unseen.

The worn trail that ribboned along beyond the back gate was rutted and uneven, mostly hard-packed dirt with the odd sprouting of grass. O'Brien followed it west, past the whole string of similar backyards, then took his first left turn and came out onto Main Street about four hundred yards away from the hotel.

Crossing the street, he continued straight down the facing alley, his first left and began to head back the way he'd come, this time on a course that would bring him out behind the dentist's surgery.

The sounds issuing from the club-room told him when he was just about to reach his destination. Laughter, the clink of glasses, a Pianola playing to the air pressure dictated by the perforations in its paper roll. O'Brien moved in closer to the rough timber fencing to his left, craning his neck just a little so that he could study the dentistry upstairs for any sign of trouble.

The place was apparently lifeless.

O'Brien reached the corner where the back-alley fed out into the side one. Hugging the fence, he chanced a look around it. A narrow set of stairs led up to the surgery entrance, but the alley itself was empty save for the constantly shifting pattern of life going by out on Main Street.

O'Brien flipped the restraining thong off his holster and took out the .38 calibre double-action Lightning, checking to make sure that it was in good working order. Then, re-sheathing the weapon, he stepped into the side alley and took the stairs two at a time, pausing to one side of the pebbled glass door to listen for sounds from within.

Nothing. Still, that was hardly surprising—provided the 'Closed' sign hanging on the door could be believed, of course.

Reaching out, O'Brien closed one fist round the door handle. After a pause he twisted it. The door cracked open. He followed it in with his guts wound as tight as a two-dollar watch.

He found himself in a small, green-walled waiting-room. He was alone. At one end sat four odd ladder-back chairs, at the other a desk, a file cabinet and a low, glass-fronted chiffonier filled with medicaments—carbolic salve, ether, chloral hydrate, phenol. A door in the opposite wall was marked 'Surgery'; O'Brien went across to it, cursing once when he hit a loose floorboard. This door, too, was half-wood, half-pebbled glass, so he was careful to stay to one side of it.

Holding his breath, he listened but heard nothing, no dialogue, no clink of instruments in dishes, no moaning or spitting up from any unfortunate patients.

Maybe the place really *was* closed.

Then a tingle washed across his sun-bronzed face as he picked out the sound of someone humming on the other side of the door.

Straightaway he thought of J P Riley; as far as he could make out, it was the same lewd but presently-popular ditty the broken-faced gunman had been humming thoughout his encounter with Goodlight.

O'Brien's hunch had proved correct, then. Riley was definitely in there, over by the window, watching the hotel with most probably a rifle in hand or nearby.

But who was in there with him? The dentist, certainly; his assistant, too, if he had one.

O'Brien didn't want to put them in any more danger than he had to. But he sure as hell wanted to lock horns with Riley.

Suddenly a scuffling issued from inside the room and O'Brien stiffened, reaching for his Colt. Then a voice interrupted the humming. It was a man, his tone strained and afraid.

'How long do you—?'

Riley: 'Shut up.'

A woman, middle-aged by the sound of her. 'But we only want to know—'

'Just shut up, stay out of the way and you won't get hurt.'

Silence again; then more humming.

O'Brien tried to pinpoint the voices on the other side of the door. Riley was almost certainly over by the window. The man and the woman were at the opposite end of the room.

Good.

Now all he had to do was find a way of dealing with Riley before the sonofabitch could start shooting and possibly kill someone.

He scanned his own surroundings, hoping for inspiration, and struck lucky. A minute later he was about as ready to brace Goodlight's gunman as he would ever be.

For a moment he listened to the distant sounds of merrymaking that drifted up from the club-room below. Gradually his pulses settled down and his breathing came naturally and without effort. He was ready.

Taking a pace back and lifting his right leg, he booted the surgery door open. There was a splintery crack and the portal shuddered inwards. As O'Brien bulled into the room, the woman over by the bookcase to his left screamed and the man in the white jacket and glasses reached out to grab her.

Ignoring them, O'Brien wheeled around to face J P Riley, who was just coming up out of a chair he'd positioned over by the window.

Riley had been sitting with a Henry repeater balanced on his lap. O'Brien saw the surprise clearly in his cold black eyes and felt a sudden fiery sense of triumph that he'd caught the would-be bushwhacker completely unawares.

Riley cried out an oath and began to bring the Henry around to hip-height. Before he could do any such unsociable thing, however, O'Brien tossed him the object he'd been holding in his left hand. The object he'd taken from the glass-fronted chiffonier before launching his attack.

A *jug of ether.*

'Catch,' he advised drily.

The look on Riley's punch-bag of a face was one of confusion and near-panic. It was all too obvious that he didn't know what to do for the best. But with O'Brien pushing past the awful-looking dentist's chair with murder in his eyes, he decided to disregard the jug.

Shame.

The container hit the floor and smashed with a tinkle, splashing the anaesthetic mixture of alcohol and sulphuric acid right over his boots. Even as his finger tightened on the Henry's trigger the vaporous but invisible cloud billow-ed up around him, making him gag and choke.

O'Brien, holding his breath, stepped in fast and yanked the rifle from his grasp. Riley yelled again, this time giving in to panic. His eyes watered freely, his mouth opened and closed again and again as he tried to find some fresh air.

Tossing the long-gun aside, O'Brien grabb-ed him by the shirt-front and yanked him around. Just before he punched Riley in the face he saw the dentist and his lady friend hightail it from the room. Then his knuckles met Riley's jaw and Riley stumbled backwards, already as dopey as all get-out from the ether he'd inhaled.

Still, the gunman wasn't finished yet. Grab-bing hold of the dentist's chair to stop himself from spilling back any further, he reached for his Remington Number 3 and O'Brien, who wanted to avoid swapping lead if at all possible, snatched up the first weapon he could find to dissuade him.

It was a scalpel used to slice gums when draining abscesses.

O'Brien threw it like a knife and it tumbled end over end across the eight feet that separated them, a short, flat and wickedly sharp instrument of dull silver, and Riley screamed when it embedded itself in his right bicep.

While he was still yelling and trying to pluck up the courage to pull the surgical knife free, O'Brien scooped up a kidney-dish from the same portable table he'd taken the scalpel, and hit Riley square in the face with it.

The dish vibrated in his hand and Riley stopped screaming. O'Brien hit him again and the cold dish fairly sang with the impact. Riley stumbled backwards with blood beginning to waterfall from his nose, and went down in a tangle of arms and legs, the scalpel still stuck fast.

O'Brien stood over him, waiting for him to get up again. But the ether and the kidney-dish had done their work well. Riley was sleeping like a baby.

Turning away from him, O'Brien went to the

window, opened it wide and stuck his head out to get some clean air. Downstairs town life went on undisturbed by the combat. He left the window open in order to clear away the smell of the anaesthetic, then quit the surgery before the law—whom he was certain the dentist and his secretary had gone to summon—could arrive.

With luck he'd be long gone from Missoula by the time the local star-packer started putting two and two together—gone from Missoula and heading north to Alaska.

He collected his horse from the livery and rode up to the railroad depot on the south side of town. The one o'clock train for Tacoma was already in and Roddy Bruce-Morgan and Chester Kane were waiting for him on the weathered platform.

O'Brien got his mount settled down in the horse-car and then joined his new companions in one of the Northern Pacific's passable but cramped carriages, where he pocketed a bank draft of $2250 which he intended to deposit as soon as possible before sailing from Seattle.

For a while they talked of inconsequentials, as folks often do when embarking upon long train journeys. Then a great, ear-splitting series of whistles and cries told them that the train was about to move out. Soon the high prairie plateaux typical of this part of Montana, where rose the Bitterroot Range, were flashing by beyond the dusty windows in an endless vista of greens and gold.

It was then that O'Brien decided to lean forward and ask the young Scotsman if Harvey Goodlight's name meant anything to him.

He could tell by Bruce-Morgan's expression that it did.

'Good—! Just where did you run into *him*!' he asked, frowning.

'My hotel room, about ten minutes after I left you,' O'Brien replied. Quickly and quietly he recounted Goodlight's attempt to bribe him and his subsequent run-in with J P Riley. By the end of it Chester Kane was eyeing him with new respect, although the news seemed only to have aged Bruce-Morgan.

'That's bad,' he muttered. 'I thought we'd left him behind in Port Angeles.'

'Who is he?' asked O'Brien.

Bruce-Morgan stared out the window for a while, organising his thoughts. O'Brien, seated opposite, watched him and his reflection share a worried glance.

'When I first got the idea to run supplies, ah, you-know-where,' the Scotsman said at last, leaning forward with hands clasped and elbows on knees, 'money was in short supply.

No matter which way we cut it, Ginny and I just couldn't raise enough hard cash to buy all the supplies we needed, nor hire the men to transport them. So we decided to take a third party into our venture.'

'Goodlight,' said O'Brien.

Bruce-Morgan nodded. 'He was—*is*—an entrepreneur whose name kept cropping up in the course of our enquiries.

'Anyway, we arranged to meet him, and after sounding him out, finally put our scheme to him. To say that he was interested would be something of an understatement. He put up the money we needed, making himself an equal partner, and we went ahead and bought both the supplies and the cattle.

'But then something happened, I'm not sure what. One of his other ventures collapsed and he lost a substantial sum of money. I presume that after that he got cold feet. He told me that he had reconsidered our deal and wanted his share of the money back.'

'Could he do that?'

'Of course. No contracts had been signed, there was nothing in writing.' A smile touched the Scotsman's lips. 'It's not that sort of deal, is it?'

'So what happened?'

'I paid him back,' Bruce-Morgan replied

simply. 'Ginny and I wired our attorneys back home to put some of our property in Ayrshire up for sale. Should have done that in the first place, I guess. Anyway, we got the money. I paid Goodlight back and that, I thought, was that.'

'But it wasn't.'

'No, it most certainly was not! Goodlight evidently gave the matter some more thought and took independent advice. He began to see that my plan was sure-fire, and that he'd been a little too hasty in pulling out. He tried to get back in again, but of course by then we no longer needed him. He hasn't given up, though. He obviously followed Chester and myself here, and through us, contacted *you*.'

'Well, he still doesn't know where you're keeping your wagons and cattle, if that's any consolation,' O'Brien said, sitting back. 'And if we can move fast enough, we'll be long gone before he gets another chance to find out.'

Bruce-Morgan nodded absently, but it was obvious that Harvey Goodlight's tenacity was worrying him. Worrying him *bad*.

The trip went pretty much to Chester Kane's timetable. The train ploughed on through the high country and on into nightfall and beyond, stopping at just about every town from Boise to Bonneville.

They rolled into Tacoma, Washington, sometime around three o'clock the following afternoon, grabbed a late lunch and then set about securing passage aboard the next stage north. The twenty-five-mile trip to Seattle took about two hours. O'Brien followed the coach trail on horseback, giving his deep-chested mount a chance to stretch its legs.

Seattle turned out to be a thriving port-city on the hilly strip of land between Puget Sound and Lake Washington, at the foot of an impressive white-topped alp Bruce-Morgan called Mount Rainier. As a centre of trade, O'Brien considered it to be as busy as San Francisco, some five or six hundred miles further down the coast. Everywhere he looked he saw signs of activity and commerce, despite the lateness of the hour. The streets and harbour area were fairly jammed with loggers and fishermen, shipbuilders and farm-workers.

'Whereabouts are you camped?' he asked as they all headed along Stewart Street towards the livery stable at which Bruce-Morgan and Kane had left their own horses a couple of days before.

'Not far,' the Scotsman replied. 'But far enough, if you get my drift. A grassy hollow protected on three sides by hills and timber about seven, eight miles east of town.'

Reaching the stable, Bruce-Morgan took possession of a finely-boned calico mare and Kane got busy saddling his own somewhat aggressive *grulla*. When they were all set, Bruce-Morgan led them east along Olive Way, then right into Boren Avenue before finally hitting open country.

By the time they reached the perimeter of the camp full dark was just about upon them, and without waiting to be told, Kane went on ahead to forewarn the men assigned guard-duty of their impending arrival.

Glancing around, O'Brien saw bare-branched trees rising dark against dark to either side of them, and smelled the faintest aroma of cooking meat on the chilly breeze. Bruce-Morgan led him around a wide curve. In the moon's pale light he saw flower-dotted slopes shelving away to left and right. Another twist in the trail; the lonesome call of a hungry wolf attracted by the meat-smell growing stronger now; another turn, the air filled only with the sound of their horses' hooves; and then O'Brien saw the uncertain orange glow of a campfire about sixty yards ahead.

As they entered the ring of light, he saw that the Scotsman had chosen his campsite well. It was a wide, flat piece of land close to a

48

shallow but clear stream. The two Conestoga wagons he'd mentioned back in Missoula sat some way off with their tongues pointed towards the North Star, and an ex-Army canvas tent stood between them. Around the fire sat three men, one of them stirring meat, potatoes and gravy in a pot above the flames, the other two spooning up more of the same from chipped enamel dishes.

Kane had already hauled his McClellan saddle from his horse's back and was leading the animal over to the makeshift rope corral just beyond the firelight. By the time he was through, Bruce-Morgan and O'Brien had dismounted and were warming themselves by the welcome blaze.

'Men,' the Scotsman said assuredly, 'I'd like you to meet the fellow I told you about a few days ago, Mr Carter O'Brien. O'Brien this is Sam Coleman, Chris Ringgold and Felipe Hermanas.'

There was a round of nods, during which a shrewd mutual appraisal took place. Coleman was a heavy-set man in stained buckskins, around his middle-fifties, with a thick white beard and deep-set blue eyes. Ringgold was somewhat younger, a big man in a heavy sailing-man's pea-jacket with a square, reliable face and spade-sized hands. Felipe Hermanas was, as his name suggested, an olive-skinned Mexican, about twenty-five or so, with a dazzling smile and a shock of shining blue-black hair. In time O'Brien would learn that Coleman and Ringgold had been hired on as wagon-drivers, and that Hermanas was one of Bruce-Morgan's four cowboys.

'Coffee?' Coleman invited after a moment.

'Make it a bucketful,' Kane replied, coming over.

Bruce-Morgan asked his men if they'd had any trouble in the last couple of days. In the distance, the night silence was broken by the odd bawling of a restless cow and the soft, comforting sound of a man singing hymns as he rode nighthawk on the herd.

'Ain't seen a soul,' Ringgold answered in what O'Brien identified as a Canadian accent. 'Why? Your Mr Goodlight been making ructions again?'

'Nothing that O'Brien here couldn't handle,' Bruce-Morgan replied. As he accepted a cup of coffee he went on, 'Still, we should be gone from here before he can make any more trouble. Ches—you and I will ride back into town again tomorrow and see what we can do about chartering a schooner. If things go to plan, we should be leaving for Alaska the day after tomorrow.'

50

'I dreenk to that,' Hermanas said, lifting his own mug.

A new thought suddenly occurred to Bruce-Morgan. 'Where's my sister?' he asked.

'Here.'

They all turned as the speaker emerged from the tent to bathe in the fire's erratic, yellow-red glow. O'Brien, eyeing her through the curtain of steam coming off his coffee-mug, saw a woman of about twenty-five or six. She stood five feet eight and was dressed in a sheepskin coat over an ice-white blouse and grey, boys'-size pants tucked into sturdy brown boots. As she came closer, moving with a poise and purpose that bespoke uncommon confidence, he was able to decipher clear-cut features set in a smooth, blemish-free face; wide brown eyes, a small, straight nose and full, soft-looking lips, the whole picture framed by curly auburn hair spilling to shoulder-length.

But as she came to a halt beside her brother and all the men shucked their headgear in greeting, O'Brien felt that there was something in her haughty bearing that implied a coldness that had nothing to do with the coming Alaskan winter. Bruce-Morgan himself had proven to be a decent-enough companion, good-natured and considerate of others. His sister, however, looked to be cut from different cloth.

51

'Roddy,' she said in a deep, curiously mordant tone, reaching over to plant a perfunctory kiss on her brother's ruddy cheek. Then she turned her attention to O'Brien and the Scotsman quickly made introductions.

'O'Brien, this is my sister Imogen. Ginny, this is—'

'Yes,' she interrupted sharply. 'Quite.'

O'Brien nodded how-do and took Ginny's extended right hand. It felt cool to the touch. Their eyes met and his initial opinion was reinforced. Here was a beautiful but unapproachable woman who knew exactly what effect she had on men and despised them for it.

'You come highly recommended, Mr O'Brien,' she said.

He smiled. 'So your brother tells me.'

They traded stares for a moment more, until the silence between them grew so awkward that Bruce-Morgan felt compelled to indicate the pot bubbling away over the flames and say, 'That smells good, Sam,' just to change the subject.

'There's plenty left,' Coleman replied, scratching at his white beard. 'Grab a plate an' dig in.'

All of them being pretty hungry by that time, they needed no second urging; all that was, save Ginny, who, having appeared long

enough to welcome her brother home, prompt-
ly turned on her heel and strode purposefully
back to her tent.

THREE

O'Brien rolled out of his blankets early next morning and went to wash down at the stream while the sky was still slush-grey. Around him the camp lay immobile, the sharp, pre-dawn air peaceful save for the odd snort or cow-bellow.

This early, the water was still cold enough to take his breath away, but he guessed it was going to be a lot colder than that where they were heading. Suppressing a shiver, he opened his war-bag and took out his razor and lather-stick, then paused. Might be wiser to quit shaving for a while, he decided. A beard would come in handy in Alaska.

By the time he got back to camp, Coleman had set a fire going and was heating up some coffee. It appeared that the buckskin-clad wagon-driver was also the expedition's unofficial cook.

'Mornin',' the older man grunted, his mouth all but lost beneath his bushy white beard. 'Here.' He handed O'Brien a mug of steaming java.

54

'Thanks.'

A while later, Bruce-Morgan and Kane joined them, both stiff with the cold. With another grunt, Coleman fixed breakfast, a greasy portion of bacon, eggs and re-fried beans.

By the time the sun was climbing above the timber to the east, the rest of the Sotsman's crew, who'd come off watch or nighthawk duty around midnight, had also come alive. Just before he saddled up to ride back into town, Bruce-Morgan made the remainder of the introductions.

Tom Koch was a thin-faced Texan, around twenty-eight years old, pale-skinned and sporting a store-bought left eye. Ed Harper was a cheerful boy barely out of his teens. He had red hair and freckles, and wore no gun. And Jack Brand proved to be a quiet and possibly sour-tempered cow-nurse from Kansas whose chocolate-brown eyes were tired and cynical.

After breakfast the Scotsman and his black bodyguard rode out, leaving the camp quiet and restful. A couple of the men withdrew to play cards. Koch sat up against a wagon wheel and read from the Bible. O'Brien, figuring he wouldn't get a better chance in the next few weeks, took out his weapons, broke them down and cleaned them up.

When he had finished, Coleman offered to

show him around, beginning with the wagons, which were full to bursting with kegs, cartons and various sacks.

'One thing I will say for that Scotchman,' Coleman admitted. 'He's got his market figured out real good. These here wagons're stacked with just about ever' comestible them sourdoughs up north is likely to want—cans o'tomatoes an'beans, peaches an' rice; sacks o'flour, cornmeal an' sweetenin'; coffee, cut plug, dried fruit; salt, pepper, yeast powders an' saleratus. We got pemmican, biscuits, Edward's pree-served potatoes, tea an' cookin' grease. Hell, man, we got jus' about ever'-thin'.'

O'Brien found it easy to believe him, too. He saw boxes of cured pork, soldered tin canisters full of liquified butter, hundred-pound slabs of bacon packed in crates insulated with bran, which kept the fat from melting away, and quite a show of dried and desiccated vegetables from Chollet & Company of Paris, France.

'I sure can't think of much that he's missed,' O'Brien confessed.

Next Coleman led him up through the cottonwoods fringing the eastern slope and into the verdant bowl where Felipe Hermanas was still riding guard on Bruce-Morgan's modest herd of Herefords.

'An' these here cattle!' the wagon driver enthused. 'Ever' one of 'em worth upwards of eighteen hunnerd dollars if we can get 'em through to the Yukon bowl!'

'*If,*' O'Brien stressed in order to bring him back to earth. 'And that's just about as close as I want *anyone* to try creeping up on me, Miss Imogen.'

'Huh?' said Coleman, startled.

They turned to find Bruce-Morgan's sister about twenty feet behind them, still half-obscured by the shade of the trees. It was obvious from her posture that she had been trying to come upon them silently.

'My,' she said, laughing coolly, 'You really *are* good.'

O'Brien frowned. 'What does that mean? That you try sneaking up on every man your brother hires just to make sure he knows what he's about?'

'Not *every* man,' she replied easily, although her general manner showed no indication of a thaw. 'Just those upon whom the security of our trip depends.'

She came forward into the morning sunlight and O'Brien saw that again she favoured her white blouse and sheepskin jacket, but that today her lower half was concealed by a black divided riding-skirt.

'And it's "Ginny", O'Brien, not "Miss Imogen".'

He nodded. 'I'll remember that.'

Coleman, caught between them, shuffled his feet for a moment, awkward around such an assertive she-male, then concluded that three was a crowd. Touching his rough, work-scarred fingers to the brim of his stained grey hat he said, 'If you'll 'scuse me, ma'am...' and left them to it.

Ginny, wearing a faint but unmistakably mocking smile, quickly took his place at O'Brien's side, surveying the milling cattle ahead, and the green, jagged skyline beyond them. The Herefords bawled and jostled. O'Brien identified yearlings, bulls, steers, weaners, cows and calves among their number. A dough-gut, or dogie, came forward to eye them sidelong. Felipe Hermanas whistled to them and made sure that none strayed too far. The cattle-smell was strong this close, but Ginny didn't seem to notice it, or if she did, to mind.

'Don't you think this initiative can work?' she asked without looking up at him. 'You sounded somewhat pessimistic when you were talking with Sam just now.'

'It's not that I don't think it'll work,' he replied, watching the sure, nimble movements of the Mexican's wiry little pony as it cut in and out of the herd. 'It's just that I don't favour counting chickens before they hatch.'

'Wait and see, eh?' she said. She turned to face him and gestured to his Colt. 'You know how to use that, do you?' she enquired.

'Uh-huh.'

'Are you fast with it?'

He eyed her calmly. 'I get by,' he replied without swagger.

Sensing something glacial in his attitude, she asked bluntly, 'Do I annoy you, O'Brien?'

He met her aggressive stare and said, 'Yes.'

'Why?' she demanded. 'Because I'm coming along on this trip? Because you don't think a woman can cut it?'

He frowned. 'What's that got to do—?'

'You're just like all the rest,' she spat, turning to face him head-on with her fists on her hips, spoiling for a fight with a man she hardly knew. 'No doubt you believe that women, like children, should be seen and not heard, and chain themselves to their pie-safes. Am I right?'

Much to her chagrin, he reached out with one hand and gently knocked her back a pace. With her face growing steadily more crimson she said, 'What was that for?'

His smile was cool, like the snow-capped

59

summit of Mount Rainier. 'I was just trying to knock that chip off your shoulder,' he replied evenly.

They locked stares for a moment, O'Brien unable to read either her expression or the emotions stirring in her wide brown eyes. 'Then she looked away, back across the shifting sea of Herefords, allowing the colour to drain slowly from her cheeks.

'Listen, ma'am,' he began softly. 'I don't know what your problem is—'

'*Problem?*' she echoed in a high, indignant tone.

'Yeah, *problem,*' he continued steadily. 'And it's not my business to enquire. But just so's we understand each other—I figure you've got the right to go any-damn-where you please and do any-damn-thing you like. All I ask in return is one thing.'

She refused to look at him. 'What?' she asked after a while.

'That you remember this,' he replied. 'There's no *you* on this trip, just like there's no *them*. There's only an *us*. Meaning we're all in it together, Ginny.' He drew in a breath, and following Coleman's example, touched his hat brim. 'Might make things easier if you bear that in mind.' He turned to go, then stopped as she called his name. 'Yes'm?'

60

She shook her head. 'Nothing.'

He shrugged. 'As you will.'

Then he continued back to camp.

The rest of the day passed without incident until Bruce-Morgan and Kane returned to camp around mid-afternoon. The Scotsman had chartered a schooner he said, a fine, seaworthy vessel called the *Vancouver Belle*—but there was more.

'What do you mean?' Ginny demanded sharply.

'I'm not sure,' he said, running one splay-fingered hand through his short black hair. 'But I think we were spotted.'

'Spotted?' It was Ed Harper, the young red-head.

'And followed,' Bruce-Morgan went on. 'By one of Harvey Goodlight's men, a rather surly fellow by name of Benteen. Remember him, Ginny?'

The Scotsman's sister nodded slowly. 'Yes, I remember him. Are you sure it was the same man?'

'As sure as I could be in the circumstances,' Bruce-Morgan replied. 'The port was pretty crowded, as you can imagine, but I saw him clearly for just a second, then he was gone. But he was looking straight *at* me, Ginny. There

61

was no way he could have failed to recognise me.' He paused, his ruddy face assuming a worried look. 'Goodlight *knew* we'd have to show up at the docks sooner or later, so he probably posted some of his men to watch out for us. Damn! That's twice I've underestimated him. You'd think I'd have learned my lesson the first time!'

'But if you only saw Benteen for a second,' Ginny persisted, 'what makes you think you were followed?'

O'Brien provided the answer. 'What would you have done if you'd wanted to get your hands on these supplies but didn't know where to find them?'

The girl nodded, taking the point. 'Follow the people who could lead me to them,' she said.

' 'sides which,' Kane said, drawing back his shin-length duster to haul a short-barrelled .476-inch Eley from leather, 'I jus' got me a feelin'—and mah feelin's is seldom wrong.'

'What're we gonna do, then?' asked Tom Koch with concern.

'We'd be sitting ducks if we tried to move out now,' O'Brien muttered, his mind already busy formulating a plan of action.

'We best stay an' fight, then,' Kane replied, his usually sombre brown face splitting in a grin. He checked the loads of the Eley, then eased it back into leather, patting the distinctive rubber grips with their eagle's-head motif. 'Right?'

'If it comes to fighting, yeah,' O'Brien agreed. He turned to the others and was suprised to find that the only face not registering any kind of apprehension apart from Kane's was Ginny's. 'Assuming you *were* followed,' he mused, 'I don't think Goodlight'll make play for your supplies until after dark. The only way in or out of here is that trail directly ahead, so he'd be a fool to try it any sooner.

'You three,' he said, indicating Harper, Koch and Brand, 'keep an extra close eye on the cattle tonight. If it comes to shooting, they'll spook bad and you'll have to hold 'em in check. Felipe, you'll have to do the same for the horses.'

'*Si, senor.*'

'Sam, Chris—you know how to shoot?'

' 'Course,' said Ringgold.

'You'll each take a wagon apiece, then. Dig in beneath each one and make sure you've got plenty of ammunition. If Goodlight *does* try something, and his men get past me and Kane, it'll be up to you.'

'Got it,' said Coleman.

'What about us?' Bruce-Morgan asked.

'O'Brien indicated the tent. 'Get in there and stay low. Goodlight's men get past us and it looks as if your drivers're having a hard time of fighting 'em back, give 'em a hand. Otherwise, stay out of it.'

'But—'

'If anything happens to you two.' O'Brien explained simply, 'we'll have no-one to guide us or handle the business when we get up north.'

'He's right,' Kane agreed with a nod. 'You two gotta stay healthy for the good o'th'expedishun.'

Bruce-Morgan's shoulders sagged. He'd been game to offer help if things got rough, O'Brien thought, but he was no fighter. His world was one of ledgers and paperwork, not blood and bullets. 'All right,' he said. 'I guess you're right.'

'Kane,' O'Brien said, starting towards his saddle-gear, where his Winchester was located. 'Grab a long-gun, some jerky and a canteen of water. Then we'll go find ourselves a cosy little vantage-point or two.'

Together the two men followed the winding trail west until the camp lay far behind them.

'Goodlight'll do it in one of two ways,' O'Brien decided. 'He'll either come in sometime around midnight, when he's sure we'll all be asleep, or he'll wait until just before dawn, when he thinks we'll least expect him.'

'I go wi' that,' Kane agreed, keeping his eyes busy. He too favoured a Winchester. His was a beautifully-maintained Model 73, for which he kept the ammunition in the bandolier slung left-to-right across his chest. 'What do you suggest we do about it?'

'Take turns keeping watch, two hours on, two hours off, otherwise we'll be too tired to fight.'

'Awright. I'll take fust watch.'

'You've got it.'

They found a dense thicket about a hundred yards from camp and settled down to wait. The location not only gave them decent cover, it also offered the advantage of high ground. They would see anyone coming along the trail long before anyone saw them, and when the time came to resist any attack Goodlight might launch, they'd be able to shoot down on their assailants from an elevation of about twenty-five feet.

It was around five o'clock now, and the sky was just beginning to lose some of its blue. Birds sang and a cool breeze blew, but each of the men might just as well have been completely alone for all the notice one paid to the other.

65

Still, that suited O'Brien, because although he was a fighting man by profession he took no pleasure in acts of violence, and thoughts of the combat this night might bring preoccupied him.

As did Ginny.

The woman was a mystery to him. She had beauty, intelligence, courage and confidence. And yet the bitter poison of hate made her unattractive and unapproachable. As he chewed on a mouthful of jerky, he wondered why that should be. That she wanted to stand up and be counted was obvious. That she was a woman in what was predominantly a man's world was also a source of frustration to her. But these things alone didn't seem enough to have soured her so.

What else was it, then? A man? A man who had taken her heart and then broken it with such savagery that even now she saw all men as enemies, adversaries to be bested?

He didn't know, and like as not would never get to find out. And in any case, it was none of his damn' business.

By seven-thirty dusk was giving way to full dark, and feeling reasonably certain that Harvey Goodlight wouldn't attack before the witching hour, O'Brien settled down to grab some sleep.

But sleep was slow in coming. He lay there for a long while, arms folded against the growing cold, long-gun within easy reach, before he finally dozed off.

Two hours later Chester Kane shook him awake, reported nothing out of the ordinary, then took his turn at hibernating. The sky was black and star-sprinkled. A full moon threw silver radiance across the trail below. O'Brien allowed his thoughts to drift back to camp. He pictured Coleman and Ringgold, belly-down beneath the wagons; Harper, Koch and Brand keeping order among the restless, bawling cattle; young Felipe Hermanas riding shotgun on the horses; and the Bruce-Morgans sitting tight in their tent. Then he thought about the bank draft in his jacket pocket. If things went the way he expected them to, he'd start earning his money tonight.

Come eleven-thirty he allowed Kane to sleep on. He knew he wouldn't find slumber easy now, so he might just as well allow the black man to rest a while longer. At one a.m Kane woke up, took over the watch duty and O'Brien stretched out to stare up at the sky.

He must've dozed off somewhere along the line, because the next thing he knew, Kane had set one hand against his shoulder and was shaking him gently.

'They heah,' he whispered.

O'Brien came up into a crouch with his Winchester grasped firmly in his fists. 'Where?'

'Still 'bout sixty, seventy yards away,' Kane replied. 'An' comin' in a-foot. That's how I knowed they was out there in the fust place— by the sound they made dismountin'.'

O'Brien nodded, glancing up at the position of the stars and the moon, which told him about three hours had passed. He'd been right, then; with dawn no more than an hour or so away, Goodlight had decided to make his move.

'Soon as we see 'em, I'll call out a challenge,' O'Brien said softly. 'Whatever happens after that's up to them.'

'Yo.'

The seconds stretched into a minute. Nothing stirred, nothing moved. Then O'Brien stiffened. He couldn't be sure, but he thought he'd seen a shadow move down on the trail. He strained his eyes to catch it again, but couldn't. Maybe he'd been mistaken. Maybe it was just his mind playing—

It wasn't.

He saw the shadow again, clearer this time. It was a man, moving cautiously along the trail, moonlight dripping off the repeater he held across his chest.

One man. Two men. Three. Six... Ten. O'Brien swallowed a sigh.

They were coming fanned out in a loose line, virtually soundless, all of them loaded for bear. Kane saw them too. Slowly he raised his '73 to his shoulder and drew a bead on the man in the lead. Beside him, O'Brien watched them come closer... closer... closer. Then, when they were no more than fifty feet away and he was certain there were no stragglers bringing up the rear, he yelled.

'Hold it! That's far enough! One more—'

But before he could finish his ultimatum, the man in the lead wheeled around, startled, and let off a deep, booming shot.

That was a cue for the bloodbath to begin.

No sooner had the first detonation shattered the stillness than Kane started returning fire. The black man's first bullet hit the leader of the would-be thieves square in the chest. The man screamed and flung his rifle up in the air. Kane's second bullet blew his jaw off and he crumpled.

Now the trail below was a firework display of muzzle-flashes. Lead tore through the night, snapping branches and shredding leaves all around them.

Both men went down on their stomachs and slithered away from the thicket, O'Brien going east, Kane west. Ten hectic seconds later O'Brien came up onto one knee, snap-aimed and blew a barrel-chested man into the hereafter with a shot that all but exploded his belly.

Down on the trail the firing tailed off some as Goodlight's men started beating a hasty retreat. Kane shot another of them in one leg. The man went over, came back up and continued on his way, alternately hopping, then limping.

O'Brien watched them go, then levered another shell into his .44/40. He had no stomach for shooting men from ambush but he knew he had to sting the sonsofbitches down there bad to make them think twice before trying the same dirty trick again.

A shortish man whose hat had come off turned his face toward the slope. The moonglow illuminated features that were forty-plus and heavily-weathered. The man held two guns and was peppering the shadows with a barrage of lead. As dispassionately as he could, O'Brien drew a bead on him, squeezed the trigger and watched him corkscrew earthward, screaming out and clutching a shattered right shoulder.

After that the gunfire grew even more sporadic, until it died altogether. O'Brien and Kane hunkered in the darkness, listening to the pounding of the gunmen's boots against the hard-packed dirt. A moment later came a few confused yells, a couple more gunshots, the jingle of harness, the whinny of spooked horses, then a wild tattoo of hooves, heading back the way they'd come at a fast clip.

Two seconds ticked into history. Then O'Brien called out softly, 'Kane?'

'I'm heah.'

'Go take a look around, make sure they've all gone. I'll check on the ones they left behind 'em.'

'Yo.'

Straightening up, O'Brien released his pent-up breath. To the east, just above the fringe of the timber, the sky began to show the faintest watery grey of dawn. A new day was breaking, he thought. But the two bodies sprawled stiffly on the trail below would never get to see it.

'Know either of 'em?' O'Brien asked.

Roddy Bruce-Morgan looked down at the bodies O'Brien and Kane had hauled back to camp ten minutes earlier. Although the light was still poor this early, the nearness of death made the Scotsman blanch. Setting his jaw, he forced himself to peer closer, looking from one corpse to the other.

'No,' he husked at last.

71

'So neither man is this feller you called Benteen?'

'No. I've... I've never seen either of these men before. They were obviously no more than hired guns.'

Chris Ringgold stumped over with a shovel in his large, blunt-fingered hands, eyeing the blood-splashed bodies without noticeable repulsion. 'You finished with 'em now?' he asked, addressing O'Brien.

'Why?'

'Figured we'd bury 'em a ways back from the trail before movin' out.'

'Forget it,' O'Brien replied. 'We're taking them into town with us. Gonna drop 'em off at the local star-packer's office.'

'Huh? But—'

'If we bury the bodies here and keep quiet about what happened last night, it'll make *us* look like the guilty parties,' the fighting man explained. 'And Goodlight's just sneaky enough to find a way of using that against us.' He shook his head. 'No, we'll keep as much as we can above-board. We don't have to muddy the water by mentioning Goodlight by name. That'll hold us up. We'll just say that these two and a few others tried to rob us last night and we fought 'em off. After all, it's no lie.'

Ginny, who had been standing a few yards

away, came closer. Although she, too, seemed unaffected by the presence of death, O'Brien noticed that she did not allow her hazel eyes to linger overlong on the bodies. 'I do believe you're right, O'Brien,' she said. 'Chris—wrap each body in a blanket and tie it to one of the spare horses. We'll deliver them to the authorities, as O'Brien says.'

Ringgold glanced at Bruce-Morgan, who nodded, then returned his gaze to Ginny. 'Yessir, ma'am.'

'Anything else?' Bruce-Morgan asked.

O'Brien shook his head again. 'Just leave all the talking to me and Kane,' he replied. 'Then, once we've squared things away with the law, we can see about boarding the *Vancouver Belle.*'

The campsite became a hive of activity as Bruce-Morgan's men prepared to move out, and O'Brien, who always travelled light, sat his horse at the mouth of the grassy bowl, watching the animation with anticipation firing his guts.

When Kane rode across to him some time later, he was leading a stiff-legged grey mule, all head and ears. 'What you want to take— lookout or drag?' the black man enquired.

'Lookout,' O'Brien replied.

Kane shrugged. 'Awright. I bring up the rear, chew all that dust.'

73

O'Brien turned his attention to the canvas-wrapped bundles strapped to the mule. 'What the hell have you got there?' he asked.

Kane hipped around in his McClellan in order to follow his gaze. When he turned back, he was grinning fiercely. 'Jus' a little keepsake from mah Army days,' he replied easily. But more than that he would not divulge.

Thirty minutes later everyone was ready to move out, and sitting astride his calico mare at the end of the column, Bruce-Morgan threw one last look at the gathering behind him.

'Ready?' he asked, glancing at his sister, who was seated beside Coleman on the first wagon.

Ginny nodded firmly. 'Ready,' she said.

A strange, expectant silence fell across the clearing. Even the birdsong seemed muted. Around them, the world was holding its breath.

Finally the Scotsman brought one hand up, then swung it forward.

'*Yah!*' yelled Coleman, slapping his reins across the backs of the horses pulling his wagon.

'*Yah!*'

'*Get along there!*'

'*Yee-hah!*'

Slowly the procession began to pile out of the tree-bordered campsite, following the winding trail back west, towards Seattle; O'Brien riding out ahead, blue eyes peeled for trouble; Bruce-Morgan next in line; Coleman and Ginny on the first wagon; Ringgold driving the second, with the two dead men on horses tied to the tailgate; then the cattle, one hundred and fifty head of slow-moving bawling Herefords, with the four cowboys riding point, swing, flank and drag on them; and finally Chester Kane, his own dark eyes as watchful as O'Brien's, his stocky grey mule trotting dutifully behind him, carrying its mysterious burden, the black man's so-called Army 'keepsake'.

FOUR

It wasn't as hard to settle things with the Seattle
sheriff as O'Brien had feared. The lawman,
a tall, skinny old bird with hard, steel-grey
eyes behind round, wire-framed spectacles,
recognised both bodies as soon as he saw them,
identifying them as a pair of crooked low-lives
well-known to the authorities.

'They tried to rob you, huh?' said the sheriff.
He grunted. 'Well, I'm not a bit surprised,
knowin' 'em of old. They had thievery in their
blood, those two. Allus knew they'd come to
a sad end one day. And what do you know?'
He smiled. 'They did.' He rummaged on his
desk, came up with some forms and had
O'Brien and Kane make out statements per-
taining to the events of the night before. Then
he counter-signed each one, rubber-stamped
them and stuck them in a desk drawer. 'All
right, get along now.'

'You mean that's *it?*' Kane asked, surprised.

'Sure, that's it,' the sheriff replied. 'I got no
reason to doubt what you've told me, not
knowing the deceased as I did. But next time,

try to cripple, not kill, huh? It saves the county coroner a whole heap o'work.'

Remounting outside, the two men retraced their steps to the wagons and cattle, which they'd left not far from Pier 51. After that, it was a small matter to herd everyone along the crowded docks that overlooked Elliott Bay, until they located the *Vancouver Belle,* moored out by Pier 59.

Although he hailed from land-locked Colorado, O'Brien had long been fascinated by the sea, and he found the fishy, salt-sharp air as pleasurable as he did the squawking of gulls and the cries of stevedores. As he stared out at the choppy grey waves, Bruce-Morgan rode up beside him and pointed out the *Vancouver Belle.*

It was, as he had said, a seaworthy enough vessel, rising and falling to the motion of the restless water, and O'Brien eyed it critically. The schooner appeared in a good state of repair, freshly painted and broad of beam. It stretched about a hundred and forty feet from bow to stern, and it had three masts heavy with off-white canvas sails snapping briskly in the wind. Smaller sails were rigged fore and aft; they too shivered and trembled to the force of the gusts. Bruce-Morgan, it appeared, had chosen their barque well.

'What now?' the Scotsman asked, raising his voice to be heard above the surrounding clamour.

O'Brien turned to face him. 'Get everyone aboard,' he replied. 'And once the horses're settled down, see if one of the men can rig up some slings to fit under their bellies.'

Bruce-Morgan frowned. 'Slings? Whatever for?'

O'Brien ran a palm along his own mount's sleek neck. 'Happen a man feels queasy, all he's got to do to make himself feel better is sick up,' he said. 'But for a horse it's not so simple. A horse *can't* vomit. So if it gets seasick, it's got no way to make itself feel better. Least we can do is try to make 'em more comfortable, and a sling under their bellies'll help support 'em during the voyage. That way they won't feel so lousy.'

Bruce-Morgan nodded his understanding. 'Good thinking. I'll have Sam Coleman figure something out. Where will you be?'

O'Brien drew his bank draft from his pocket. 'Depositing this,' he replied.

'All right,' said the Scotsman. 'We'll see you in a little while.'

Three hectic hours later, the *Vancouver Belle* was finally ready to sail. The two Conestogas were lashed tight to her foredeck and covered

with tarpaulins, and the cattle were safely in-
stalled in a crude but sturdy pen erected at the
stern. The horses, taken below to the cargo
hold, were rigged up much as O'Brien had suggested, with wide, double-folded strips of canvas hung under their bellies and fastened to the
low ceiling above to ease the often-nauseating
roll of a ship at sea.

The skipper of the *Belle* was a short, pot-
bellied old sea-dog by the name of Barnabas
Collins. Dressed in a dark-blue uniform and
matching peaked cap, the captain had a seamed, fiftyish face and a thick black beard marbled with grey. He struck O'Brien as a reliable
sort, square-faced, brown-eyed, leather-lipped
and direct. When he was sure they were ready
to sail, he called orders down to the first mate,
and the first mate directed them on to the rest
of the crew.

The schooner's sails were unfurled. Almost
at once they filled with wind. O'Brien listened
to the yells and cries of the crew at work, the
creak of stretching guy lines, the metallic *clank-
clank* of the anchor chain being wound up.
Bells and sirens met his ears, then lost themselves in a cacophony of other sounds. Whistles
blew. The cattle bawled. Then the *Vancouver
Belle* began to steam regally away from Pier 59,
slowly at first, her entire frame shuddering

79

beneath his feet.

Across Elliott Bay she went, passing passenger ships and tramp steamers just coming in from the north. O'Brien peered back at Seattle's ragged skyline, seeing factory chimneys spewing black smoke into the cloudy sky. He smelled it acrid on the chilly air as they slowly cruised past Edmonds and out into the Strait of Juan de Fuca, trending westward now, past Port Angeles, on their left.

After a while he grew aware of someone standing beside him on the larboard, or port, side of the schooner, and looking down, met Ginny's forthright gaze.

'Well,' she said. 'We're on our way at last.'

'Yes'm,' he said politely.

He leaned forward, setting his elbows on the wooden bulwark. Beneath them, the grey waves pushed away from the ship in a series of bubbling white-tops. Up in the wheelhouse, which was set amidships, Bruce-Morgan watched Captain Collins' every movement with almost childlike fascination. The rest of the men were scattered around them, laughing and joking with the crew.

At this point the channel was about twelve miles wide, and the skipper was keeping his vessel on a steady course straight down its middle. The Pacific Ocean still lay some fifty miles away; meanwhile, they could still just about see land.

It was thinking of distances that made O'Brien ask, 'How far is this place your brother intends to dock at?'

'Yacutat?' Ginny replied. 'Oh, about five or six hundred miles.'

'How long do you figure it'll take us to reach it?'

She considered. 'Ten days?' she said speculatively. 'Certainly no more than a fortnight. Why? You don't get seasick, do you?'

O'Brien smiled. 'No ma'am,' he said. 'But I can think of someone who *does*.'

Following his line of vision, she focused on Chris Ringgold, who was bent double over the railing about thirty feet away emptying his stomach into the heaving deeps.

'Oh dear,' the girl said, with more amusement than sympathy.

In the circumstances, O'Brien too found himself lightening up. Above them, wide-winged seagulls swooped around the rigging, and the wind, now carrying icy droplets of spray, had turned decidedly bitter.

'I don't know about you,' he said, addressing the girl, 'but I could sure use a mug of hot coffee right about now. What say we go down to the saloon-room and get one?'

She eyed him oddly, as if she were trying to divine the real reasons for his invitation. Without thinking about it, she took half a pace away from him, icing up again. 'I...' Her tongue appeared briefly to moisten her full lips. 'No thank you, O'Brien,' she replied formally. 'I...I think I'll stay on deck for a while.'

His attempt to suppress a sigh of mingled puzzlement and annoyance failed. After all, he was only trying to be friendly. What was wrong with her? Didn't she want that? Was she *afraid* of men? Was *that* the reason for her strange behaviour? 'As you will,' he said, nodding. 'Maybe I'll see you later.'

'Maybe.'

He turned away and headed for the narrow door that led downstairs to the saloon-room. Behind him, Ringgold let go another batch of half-digested food.

As it turned out, the cramped saloon-room, with its mahogany bar, steam-filled galley and single line of natty, bolted-down writing tables, was to become the hub of their small community as the miles unwound, simply because there was nowhere else to go.

Predictably, however, Ginny spent most of her time in her stateroom, while her brother shadowed Captain Collins everywhere, keen to learn the workings of the ship. Tom Koch read his Bible or sung hymns to the queasy cattle. Ed Harper and Jack Brand played cards for matches. And as for Chris Ringgold—well, he just threw up a lot.

For his part, O'Brien spent a fair part of each day up on deck, making the most of what was, for him, a rare and pleasant experience. Overhead the sky grew slate-grey as they nosed further north. Around them the sky mirrored the colour and darkened it still further. By using his field glasses, the freelance fighting man could just about make out the misty bulk of Vancouver rising many tens of miles to the northeast, but soon a cold, persistant and stinging drizzle cut visibility by three-quarters.

On the morning of the second day, Bruce-Morgan began to express worries about the cattle. They were too exposed to the elements, he said. And now that the weather was turning that much cooler, he had to think about protecting his investment.

After much discussion Captain Collins offered him the use of two large squares of canvas, and together, O'Brien, Kane and the rest of the men rigged up some kind of roof over the livestock pen, which kept out the worst of the weather.

Three days into the voyage, with Nootka

Island about eighty miles to starboard, they ran into a band of wind-driven sleet. The squall didn't last long; just long enough to shake loose the eye-teeth of everyone aboard and convince Ringgold that he had actually died and gone to Hell.

The *Vancouver Belle* ploughed on through the throbbing waves with much creaking and groaning. Icy water burst against her bows and puddled on the foredeck. The cattle bellowed and stamped while down below the horses whinnied and rocked in their slings, believing world's-end had come.

One level up, in the cream-walled saloon-room, O'Brien and the rest of Bruce-Morgan's team drank fortified coffee and sat the storm out in silence. None of them had experienced such a tempest at sea before, and even O'Brien was beginning to feel a shade green about the gills. Grey water splashed against the portholes, affording them only a blurred view of the choppy pulsating waves beyond. Through the distorted glass it appeared that the entire world was melting.

And yet, paradoxically, the weather just kept getting colder, the sky darker, the waves taller.

To keep up their moral, young Ed Harper suggested a spot of communal crooning. He kicked off with,

84

'Oh bury me not in the deep, deep sea,
Where the dark blue waves will roll over me—'

to which Chris Ringgold growled, 'Shuddup.'

Fifteen minutes later, the squall was behind them, and the *Vancouver Belle* began to settle down once more. Soon crockery stopped rattling and tinkling in cupboards, and the creaks and groans of the schooner quietened down.

Silently thanking their gods, the Scotsman's men went up top to stretch themselves and check on the Herefords and wagons. To be honest, there wasn't one of them who hadn't thought his last moment had come—and not one of them now who wasn't more grateful than words could say to find himself still breathing the crisp, gusting air.

Half an hour later, whilst repairing part of the storm-damaged cattle-pen, Felipe Harmanas glanced up and saw a black, thick-waisted steamer chugging along in their wake.

The craft appeared to be pursuing them.

Alerted by his cry Bruce-Morgan lumbered down to the stern of the *Belle* and joined the young Mexican at the bulwark. Following his raised left hand, the Scotsman discerned the pursuing craft. Thick, dark smoke belched skyward from its twin funnels and it rode low in the water about ninety or a hundred yards away, but for all its ungainly shape it was fast, and gouging a foam-flecked path through the beating sea towards them at an alarming rate.

As Ginny came up beside him, he strained his eyes to make out its flag, but it wasn't sporting one.

'What is it?' Ginny demanded.

He turned to her. 'I don't know,' he replied, frowning. 'You'd better go and fetch—'

Before he could finish what he was going to say, a low, sharp *whump* made them all wheel back toward the black steamer. They were just in time to see the still-brisk wind wrench a cloud of smoke away from a point near the 'v' of the ship's bow.

'What—?' the Scotsman began.

But again he was interrupted, this time by a thunderous detonation which threw up a great spout of water eighty feet away from them.

'A *cannon!*' Hermanas hissed, startled.

The act of aggression meant only one thing.

'My God,' Bruce-Morgan said, turning back to Ginny. 'Pirates! Fetch O'Brien—*quickly!*'

O'Brien was down below, still seeing to the comfort of the horses, so the first he knew about this new development was when Ginny came below to find him. Together they retraced

86

their steps back up to the deck and swayed to the stern, where Bruce-Morgan, his men and a few of the captain's crew were watching the steamer chugging along behind them and a touch to their larboard side, still closing the distance rapidly.

'Pirates!' the Scotsman said when O'Brien elbowed his way to the bulwark beside him.

'That or Goodlight again,' he agreed. Twisting around, he scanned the faces behind him until he spotted their skipper. 'You know these waters better than most, captain. *Do* pirates sail these parts?'

Collins' seamed face was grim, and his marbled beard glistening with a thousand droplets of spray. 'They *have*, before now,' he replied. 'But not for many a year. The U.S Navy saw them off once, and sometimes the revenue cutters patrolling the Bering Sea sail down this far just to make sure they haven't come back.'

They all digested that.

'Chances are it's Goodlight again, then,' Kane remarked at last.

Captain Collins took a step towards the Scotsman. 'I'm warning you, Bruce-Morgan! If the freebooters in that tug yonder are anything to do with you, I'll hold you personally responsible for any damage they do to my ship!'

Nimbly O'Brien stepped between them before tempers could snap altogether. Tightly he said, 'What's our speed, skipper?'

Collins relaxed. 'Eight knots, or thereabouts,' he responded.

'Can you double it?'

The old sea-dog's brown eyes lifted to the sky as he considered. 'I can probably take it up to twelve, thirteen knots, aye,' he confessed.

'Do it, then. And quick as you can!'

'We'll never outrun 'em if that's what you're thinking,' the skipper said. 'No matter how much the wind favours us, steam's got the beating of us, as much as it pains me to admit it. Besides, that squall knocked some of our rigging loose, so we're not as fit as we should be.'

O'Brien put his eyes back on the steamer behind them. 'I'm not so much concerned with outrunning 'em,' he replied, half to himself. 'At the moment I'd settle for just staying out of range of their cannon.'

'All right,' the captain said. 'I'll do me best.' He turned and hurried back to the wheelhouse, shouting orders to the crew.

Another ominous *whump* issued from the pursuing steamer's bow. Another cloud of smoke was quickly whipped and shredded by the wind. But this time the resulting explosion

88

was no more than sixty feet off the larboard side, causing Ginny to scream and some of the men to begin muttering worriedly.

O'Brien glanced around at them. It was time to restore some order before panic turned them into so many headless chickens.

'Sam! Break out some guns. If they want to make a fight of it, we'll oblige them. But no firing until I give the word. Got it?'

'I got it.' Coleman turned to Ringgold. 'C'mon, Chris. You heard the man.'

Ringgold nodded weakly, still as pale as paper.

'Jack, you and Ed try to keep these cows from spooking any more than they already have. If they break out of this pen and run loose there'll be the devil to pay.'

'Right!'

'Felipe, when Sam gets back, you and Tom grab guns and keep 'em—'

'Pard'n me, Mr O'Brien,' said Koch, raising his right hand sheepishly.

O'Brien frowned. 'What?'

'It's no good me grabbin' a gun,' Koch replied. 'I don't fight, y'see. Never have, an' don't plan on startin' now. It's agin the Good Book.'

O'Brien bit off a curse. 'All right. Jack— you and Tom switch places. Any questions?'

'Just one,' said Bruce-Morgan. 'Ginny and I...?'

'Down below,' O'Brien replied.

The Scotsman nodded, taking his sister's arm. 'That's what I thought.'

The pirate ship, if that's what she was, loosed off another blast of cannon-fire, but again the detonation threw up a geyser of water to one side of the *Belle*.

'You know sump'n?' Kane said, coming over. 'I don't think them sonsabitches got any intentions o'hittin' us. *I* think they jus' want to *scare* us.'

O'Brien's thoughts had been running along a similar track. Whoever was aboard that evil-looking steamer wanted to show off their capabilities, in other words, *warn* them into submission. It wasn't likely that they wanted to risk damaging whatever they intended to steal.

Even so, they *might* turn nasty. And it was almost certain to come to fighting, if the captain was right, and steam *could* overtake sail.

The steamer chugged closer.

She was still about eighty yards out, but steadily drawing up to a line upon which she would run parallel to the *Vancouver Belle*. Now O'Brien could make out the hard-looking men busying themselves around the French-built but American-designed Hotchkiss gun on the bow. The weapon looked lethal and could fire two-pounder shells almost continuously if desired. But for now the pirates held back.

'Once they're alongside us, they'll start edging in closer, probably using rifle-fire to keep us pinned down,' O'Brien said angrily. 'Then, before we know it, they'll be boarding us and fighting'll be hand-to-hand.' He glanced up and down the length of the deck, the damp, salty wind whipping around his ears. 'Dammit, Kane. If only we had a cannon of our own we could give 'em a taste of their own medicine.'

Something flared in the black man's eyes and he snapped his fingers, making O'Brien study him closely and bark, 'What is it?'

Kane threw one more look at the steamer, then said, 'I got an idee. Come with me!'

He followed the black man back along the heaving ship until they came to the foredeck, to which the wagons had been firmly lashed. At once Kane bent to untie the olive-green tarpaulin which had been spread over them to weather-proof them for the duration of the voyage.

'Gimme a hand heah,' the negro said without turning around.

O'Brien crouched beside him, cold, unworkable fingers struggling with stout ropes.

91

'Morgan didn't pack a cannon along with the rest of his supplies, did he?' he enquired with more than a smidgin of gallows humour.

'Not a cannon, no,' Kane replied as the *Vancouver Belle* rose high, then slammed bow-first back into the sea, drenching them. 'But he *did* fetch along some dyn'mite.'

'*Dynamite!*'

'Sure. Figured we might need to blast our way through a snow-drift or two 'twixt heah an' the Yukon basin. An' if not, well, he c'd sell whatever was left to them sourdoughs.'

Now O'Brien's mind was racing with the possibilities the explosives offered, paramount among them the opportunity to *really* fight back. Together they yanked the tarpaulin aside and stared into the backs of the two wagons.

'Now,' Kane muttered. 'Which one...'

'You check the right, I'll check the left,' O'Brien replied quickly.

'Awright. The stuff's packed in a small wooden crate somewhere near the bottom, but you can't miss it—it's well-marked.'

Both men began rooting through the supplies, working at a feverish pace. Cans and kegs fell aside as they dug deeper into the Scotsman's wares. Then O'Brien's fingers touched the light, splintery wood of a crate. Red-painted words, CAUTION! EXPLOSIVES!

HANDLE WITH CARE, met his gaze.

'*Got it!*'

Together they lifted the box of potential death out of the wagon-bed and set it down on the slippery deck. Then, while Kane re-tied the tarpaulin, O'Brien took the crate in both arms and hustled down to the wheelhouse.

Captain Collins was still bellowing urgent orders and his men were still scurrying all over the place, unfurling more sails fore and aft and trying to effect temporary repairs to the damaged rigging.

Stopping the first mate, O'Brien said, 'I need some cord.'

'Rope?'

'Twine, if you've got it.'

The first mate pointed to a bald man with a thick beard. 'Kelly! Twine for this man!'

'Aye-aye!'

O'Brien set the box down in one corner and used his scratched-up old jack-knife to prise open the lid. Inside, wrapped in straw, he found two rows of dynamite-sticks, fourteen in all, and a coil of fuse. Glancing down at him, Captain Collins blurted an oath. 'Good grief, man, what on earth have you got there?'

'Sump'n that might jus' save yo' ass,' Kane replied, stumping in and closing the door behind him.

Here,' said the sailor named Kelly, handing O'Brien a loop of twine. 'This all right?'

'Fine. Kane, give me a hand with this, will you?'

Crouching over the crate, O'Brien took three sticks of nitroglycerine and held them together, so that, if viewed head-on, they formed a roughly triangular shape. Without having to be told, Kane took the knife, cut a length of twine and fastened the sticks together, tying them twice, once near the top, once near the bottom.

As they began to repeat the procedure, the first mate burst back in. 'They're gainin' on us, cap'n.'

'How close?'

'No more'n fifty yards to larboard!'

Collins cursed again, then sighed. 'All right, Pike. As you were.' To O'Brien he said, 'I don't know what you've got in mind, mister, but it had better work!'

O'Brien glanced at Kane, who was as beaded with sweat and spray as he was. 'You ever played baseball?' he asked.

Kane shrugged. 'A time or two.'

'Were you any good as a pitcher?'

'Fair, I guess.'

'Good,' O'Brien said, cutting down lengths of fuse for them to insert into the four bombs they'd just created. 'Come on, let's get these things outside.'

'Amen to that,' muttered Collins.

The twin-funnelled steamer had indeed gained on them. Now O'Brien saw her name clearly against the slick black wood of her bow. The *Pamela Royal*. She stood no more than forty yards off the larboard side, almost parallel to them at last, and turning by degrees to put herself on a course that would bring her close enough to send across a boarding-party.

No sooner had O'Brien and Kane appeared on the deck than a few of the pirates—although, as O'Brien now saw, they were dressed more for range-work than sea-duty—began to pepper them with rifle-fire. Crouching down behind the bulwark, they took a hasty breather.

'Whew!' said Kane. 'They mean business!'

O'Brien hefted one of the bombs. 'So do *we*,' he replied meaningfully.

Collins' men were no longer climbing the rigging; it was too dangerous for that now. The Herefords, too, seemed to be anticipating the coming confrontation. O'Brien heard it in their frightened keening. About sixty feet along the deck, Coleman, Ringgold, Hermanas and Brand were finding positions from which they could return fire.

Kane swept off his hat and chanced a look over the bulwark. 'They're gettin' closer,' he announced soberly. ' 'Nother few yards an' I figure they'll be in range.'

'Right.' O'Brien handed him two of the three-stick bundles. 'You got lucifers?'

Kane produced a waterproof tin of sulphur-tipped matches. 'Sure.'

'When they get close enough, then, give 'em hell. The more damage you can do to their hull, the better. But for God's sake watch yourself.'

'How 'bout you?'

O'Brien indicated the foredeck. 'I aim to get up front a-ways. If I can, I'm gonna take out that blasted Hotchkiss gun.'

' 'Luck,' Kane said, nodding sharply. Then they split up.

O'Brien moved along the shuddering deck on his hands and knees, the home-made bombs jammed into the pockets of his wolf-skin jacket. Behind him, gunfire dwarfed the crashing of the sea as Bruce-Morgan's men gave as good as they got.

Bullets whacked and thudded into the schooner's superstructure. O'Brien heard the captain's voice booming, 'Hard a-starboard! Hard a-starboard!' Then came more shouting, this time the eager and prematurely-triumphant kind that issued from the raiders aboard the *Pamela Royal*.

O'Brien pushed himself up to peer over the

bulwark. The steamer was fairly crashing through the waves, bearing right down on them. Maybe it was her intention to ram the *Belle* and loot her before she sank.

Quickly he gauged distances. The reinforced prow of the steamer was no more than thirty yards from the Schooner's hull now. And *that*, O'Brien decided, was just about near enough.

He went down just as a few shots whined harmlessly overhead, and reached into his pocket. The first match he struck was damp and refused to light. So was the second. The third, however, burst into flame immediately. Urgently he touched it to the fuse of his first bundle of dynamite and released a sigh when the fuse began to spark and splutter.

Gripping the nitro-sticks in his right hand, he watched the fuse burn lower, trying to time his throw just right. Despite the cold, sweat dribbled into his eyes and he squeezed them shut to clear it away.

Then, voicing a defiant cry, he came up from behind the bulwark, quickly sighted on the Hotchkiss gun bolted to the *Pamela Royal's* foredeck, and praying speedily, lobbed his bomb overarm.

The dynamite tumbled end over end through the drizzly air. The fuse guttered and fizzed. The explosives landed just beyond the cannon and blew almost at once.

O'Brien saw a sudden burst of light and heard an ear-splitting roar. Then came the screams, and a wave of tremendous heat that seared his face. About three bodies shot into the air, tumbling and disjointed, and parts of the cannon and great splintered lengths of the steamer's bow rained down from the sky to dash themselves still further against the pitiless waves.

O'Brien went down again, feeling the schooner straining in a tight turn away from the marauding ship, just as Kane's first nitropacked bomb went off, tearing into one of the *Royal*'s funnels.

Now the shouting aboard the steamer turned to cries of panic as the would-be filibusters tried to put out a dozen or more small fires. Further down the deck, Coleman and the others began doing their best to pick the pirates off with their long guns.

Kane threw his second bundle of dynamite. This one, too, exploded against the first of the funnels, toppling it slowly with a bone-freezing scream of twisting metal. Something in the hold of the pirate vessel burst with a dull crash, possibly a boiler.

O'Brien straightened up with his remaining bomb held loosely at his side, unlit. He'd guessed there'd be no further use for the dynamite and it looked as if he was right.

The steamer had virtually come to a standstill in the wind-ruffled water. The black smoke billowing into the air now came from fires beyond the boiler-room. Listing slightly to one side, the *Pamela Royal* looked badly beaten, and the men racing about on deck slipped and slid in their haste to contain the damage.

The *Vancouver Belle* began to pull away from her sharply, and Coleman and the others loosed a cheer that was more relieved than triumphant.

Bruce-Morgan and Ginny reappeared on deck, the girl flushed with excitement and her brother pale and shaky. 'My God, you two, that was incredible!' the Scotsman enthused. But his good-humour was short-lived. Frowning as he refocused on the creaking steamer now falling rapidly behind them he said, 'Are we swinging about to collect the survivors, do you know?'

Kane shook his head. 'You think they'd've swung aroun' to collect *us?*'

'But—'

'Quit fretting,' O'Brien cut in, gesturing to the pirate vessel. 'That ship's not as badly hurt as it looks. Its buccaneering days might be over, but it'll limp back to wherever it came from all right. Still...'

'What?' asked Ginny.

He shrugged. 'I'd just like to know whether or not we've got Goodlight to thank for this little donnybrook—and if we *have*, what *else* he's gonna throw at us to get his hands on your supplies.'

FIVE

The remainder of the voyage passed without incident.

The *Vancouver Belle* ploughed slowly on through the blustery Pacific, into Queen Charlotte Sound and ever northward, and life aboard the schooner settled back into its quiet, almost relaxed pattern. Repairs were effected to the damaged rigging and the canvas carried on snapping and flapping to the gusts of the chill, showery breeze.

The temperature began to drop steadily, and O'Brien dug out his old sheepskin jacket and gloves. Sleet became a regular fixture as the days rarely brightened much beyond the first grey glimmer of dawn.

Down in the saloon-room, Coleman and the cowboys played cards while Tom Koch read the Bible or went up top to sing hymns to the moaning cattle. O'Brien and Kane chatted about this and that, Kane's military career, O'Brien's years as a freelance adventurer; and as for Chris Ringgold—well, let's just say he didn't keep much down of what he ate.

To the east they passed the Baranof and Chichagof Islands, names left over from Alaska's original Russian occupancy, then sailed within sight of Cross Sound, which led into the coastal city of Juneau, where some of the most promising gold-strikes had so far been found. White ice crusted along the *Belle*'s ropes and anchor chain, dusting the deck and tarpaulins like spilt sugar.

Eleven days later, at sometime around noon, they sailed into Yacutat.

The town was nothing special, a cluster of sturdy frame buildings surrounded by the towering but mist-hidden spires of Mounts Elias and Fairweather. Its wharf was empty save for one or two fishing-boats and its streets, which were paved with wood ashes and coal cinders, might just as well have been the streets of a ghost town for all the life that showed upon them.

As the schooner drew nearer, however, fighting against the stormy waters of the Gulf of Alaska, O'Brien made out some of the town's inhabitants—fishermen, miners and a few flat-faced Indians, all of them trudging along the muddy sidewalks in awkward, wobbling gumboots. They looked like a mean bunch.

At last they docked and set about herding the cattle out of their pen. As he watched the cowboys whistle and yell to get the stubborn beasts moving, O'Brien caught the smell of herring and salmon strong on the bitter air, the fish-scents mingling with the sickly stench of whale-oil and woodsmoke.

If this was a sample of what Alaska had to offer, he told himself bleakly, then the sourdoughs could keep it.

It took a long while to get everything belonging to Bruce-Morgan off the *Belle*. By the time they'd finished, a curious crowd of about thirty people had turned out to watch them.

While Hermanas and the others drove the Herefords off the dock and into a reasonably grassy bowl of land about two hundred feet beyond the town, the wagon-drivers hitched up their team animals and slowly started the Conestogas rattling along Main Street.

Night fell early, and by the time Bruce-Morgan had found them lodgings and O'Brien had figured out a roster for guard-duty, the sky was as black as pitch and damp with drizzle.

In Yacutat's crude and over-priced hostelry, those men not assigned watch-duty until midnight ate a meagre supper of vegetable stew. The dining-room was log-built and mud-chinked, and illuminated by two guttering Rochester lamps and the erratic but nonetheless welcome glow of a fire. Now, with O'Brien and

103

the others the room's sole occupants and their landlady out back washing pots, Bruce-Morgan decided that he could speak freely.

Taking out and unfolding a fairly plain map, he urged his companions to gather around. 'We are here,' he said, indicating a spot on the upward curve of the Alaskan coastline. 'And *this* is our eventual destination; the Alaskan side of the Yukon basin.

'It lies some one hundred and seventy miles due north, at the very heart of what the people here call the Interior, and under normal circumstances we would use the waterways—the Yukon River and its main tributaries, the Porcupine, Tanana and Koyukuk—as our means of reaching trail's end. But of course, what with winter setting in, the water will soon ice up— so that route is closed to us.

'That leaves us with one alternative,' the Scotsman said, pausing for effect. 'To forge a trail overland.' Another pause. 'Need I stress that the journey before us has dangers a-plenty? The land is rugged, gentlemen, impassable in some places. And when we hit the snowfields, we're *really* going to have our work cut out for us.

'Still, I anticipate that all out endeavours will be worthwhile. Earlier on, out host told me that winter has already taken a firm grip on the

Interior, so by the time we get through, I expect those sourdoughs to be more than willing to pay top dollar for our supplies.'

'What route're we takin'?' asked Coleman.

'A straight line,' Ginny cut in. 'We'll take the supplies as far as we can by wagon, then transfer to sledge.'

'You mean switch to handlin' dogs?'

'Yes,' Bruce-Morgan nodded. 'But don't worry, we'll be hiring on some Tlingits to help out.' He glanced around at his crew. 'Any questions?'

'Who'll be guiding us?' O'Brien asked, scratching his by-now hairy chin.

'An Athabascan Indian by the name of Raven,' Bruce-Morgan replied. 'He'll be waiting for us about ten miles to the north, at a place called Stotter's Post.'

O'Brien nodded.

'Right,' said Bruce-Morgan. 'Bed down then, men, and sleep comfortably while you can. Tomorrow at daybreak we'll get you all kitted out with some good warm clothing—and then we'll be on our way.'

Next morning, as the *Vancouver Belle* prepared to sail back the way she'd come, the Scotsman fitted his men out with *mukluks* (lightweight seal-skin boots trimmed with fur) and tight-fitting *qiviut* sweaters knitted from the wool of the musk ox. Then they set about preparing for the first stage of their trek to the Interior with the breath misting before their faces.

Yacutat, it seemed, was not sorry to see them go. As the two wagons trundled down the street and the one hundred and fifty Herefords bawled and jostled along behind them, no inhabitants watched them leave, or waved, or wished them good fortune.

The tundra across which they travelled was both uneven and largely unremarkable. Tall mountains rose up to scratch at the lowering clouds, and the wrinkles in the land made their progress slow. Wild flowers—fireweed as tall as a man, clustered forget-me-nots, alpine azaleas and arctic lupines—splashed colour across the otherwise grey landscape, and the hours were enlivened only by the occasional sighting of a caribou or distant grizzly.

Ahead the terrain buckled up even more, and granite peaks rose slate against slate. The clouds looked heavy with snow, and an arctic hand ruffled the short, tufty grass.

As the morning wore on they began to follow a mountain track skyward, and O'Brien pulled back his quarter-horse in order to ride alongside Bruce-Morgan. 'This is the way to Stotter's Post, is it?' he asked.

The Scotsman nodded. 'Yes. It's an abandoned trading-station just the other side of this range.' He glanced up at the sky. 'With any luck we should reach it before nightfall.'

With a nod O'Brien dropped back still further, past Coleman's wagon, then Ringgold's, then past the Herefords, strung out in a winding brown line, until he could stirrup-up alongside Chester Kane, who was bringing up the rear with his stocky grey mule in tow.

'How goes it?' he greeted.

The black man glanced across at him. 'Dusty,' he replied, waving a hand before his face.

O'Brien took the hint. 'All right. I'll ride drag for a while and you ride lookout.'

'Yo!' The negro kicked his *grulla* into motion and O'Brien watched him go, smiling.

About half a mile further on, however, he began to get an itch between his shoulder-blades, and hipped around in the saddle to glance back the way they'd come. Although he saw nothing save empty prairie, across which their own back-trail was snaked as clear as a freshly-made scar, he just couldn't shake the feeling that they were being watched.

The trading-station was a tumbledown dwelling of raw logs set beside a sluggish stream and among waist-high weeds and flowers. They reached it at around three-thirty that same afternoon.

'Hello the house!' Bruce-Morgan called out as the small column came to a halt seventy feet away.

There came no reply.

'Raven?'

The log cabin was silent.

Few of its tar-paper windows remained intact, but its roof seemed sound enough. A rust-corroded tin stovepipe protuded from its sloping, weathered roof, and the door still hung reasonably well on its leather hinges. Beyond the place rose a few dozen Sitka spruce; beyond them lay more mountains, blue-grey and snow-capped; sleeping giants in the late afternoon gloom.

'Raven, are you in there?'

Silence.

While the rest of the column waited expectantly, O'Brien rode up beside the Scotsman, his eyes wary. 'What's wrong?' he asked.

Kane replied, twisting around in his McClellan while his *grulla* scratched impatiently at the spongy soil. 'Not sure. But for a meetin'-place, that cabin yonder sure looks deader'n a doornail.'

Scanning what remained of Stotter's Post, O'Brien had to agree. 'This Raven,' he said, addressing Bruce-Morgan. 'You're sure he arranged to meet you here and not someplace else?'

'Positive.'

'Could he have decided to hell with it?'

'Not Raven. He's not that sort of fellow. I've done business with him before. His word is his bond, O'Brien.'

O'Brien exchanged a look with Kane. The warrior instinct in both men told them that trouble was brewing. 'Think I'll take a closer look, then,' O'Brien said quietly. 'Keep your eyes peeled, Ches.'

Handing his reins to Bruce-Morgan he dismounted and drew his Winchester from its sheath. Then, holding the long-gun across his chest, he began to wade through the jungle of weeds and blue-tipped forget-me-nots toward the cabin.

A stray breeze blew up, stirring the tree-branches in the background, and one of the horses nickered. Behind him, Bruce-Morgan and the others followed his progress with baited breath, their nerves slowly pulling ever more taut.

The trading-post looked even more deserted close up. Cobwebs sketched the broken windows with thin, intricate pencil lines. Cautiously O'Brien approached the main door, and

109

standing to one side of it, reached out and pushed it open.

The leather hinges made a parched creaking sound.

O'Brien waited a few seconds, but nothing happened. He went inside and the dusty shadows ate him up.

The post's interior was just a skeleton. Everything of value, no matter how slight, had been stripped from the place and carried away over the years. The stovepipe they'd seen from outside was all that remained of the stove itself; that had been unbolted and spirited away a long time before, if the dust around the bolt-holes was anything to go by. Only a plank-and-crate counter and a few bare shelves remained.

Those, and a body.

O'Brien had been expecting something like that, but even so it shook him up some to actually find it. It was sprawled in the northwest corner, on its belly, arms and legs twisted grotesquely. He crossed the plank floor quickly, propped his rifle against one wall and kneeling, turned the corpse over.

It was a man, around forty years of age. His eyes were open but glazed, and some blood had dried on his lips. He was wearing a threadbare parka, wool pants and *mukluks*. From the colour of his flat, weathered face and the midnight blue-black of his shoulder-length hair, O'Brien placed him as an Athabascan Indian.

Raven? Almost certainly.

O'Brien examined him closer. He'd been stabbed more than once in the stomach. Blood was splashed across the front of his coat. The bruises up around his jaw and temple showed that he'd also been beaten up.

He hadn't been dead all that long.

Even as that thought occurred to him, O'Brien heard a scream from outside, and a gunshot.

What the—!

As more cries and pistol-cracks joined together he shoved himself away from the body, grabbed the Winchester and raced for the door. By the time he burst back out into the open he had a shell jacked into the long-gun's breech.

He took in the situation at once.

Bruce-Morgan's small column was under attack from a band of Athabascans dressed similar to the one back in the cabin. There were about seven of them that he could see, and they were attempting their ambush from both sides of the rugged trail.

But there was no more time to waste of the hows and whys of it. Questions would have to wait. He brought the Winchester up on a fur-

111

clad Indian racing through the tall weeds towards him. The man was short—five and a half feet, if that—and he was waving a Walker Colt around as if he wasn't quite sure how to use it; but that didn't make him any less of a danger.

O'Brien pulled the Winchester's trigger but the shot went wide. Quickly he pumped another .44/40 into the breech and tried again.

This time the Athabascan caught the bullet right in the breadbasket and flipped over backwards with a dying rasp.

O'Brien leapt over him and ran to join the fray. Up ahead he saw Chester Kane in hand-to-hand combat with an Indian wielding a fan-shaped *ulu* knife. The black man dodged one vicious swipe, then another, then caught his attacker's wrist and twisted it hard.

As the Indian's cry turned from one of war to one of pain, another of them threw himself at O'Brien from behind, trapping him in a bear-hug. But their bulky clothing wasn't designed for wrestling. O'Brien broke the hold with ease and spun around to come face to face with the man. Their eyes met for a second. Then O'Brien hit him in the nose with the butt of his long-gun.

The Athabascan went down without so much as a whisper.

By now the fighting was almost over. Kane had dispatched his adversary with a bullet from his Eley. Old Sam Coleman used a Sharps Big Fifty to blow most of another Indian's guts into the man racing along behind him and Felipe Hermanas stopped one more with his .45. The rest—no more than two warriors—began to stagger and stumble back up the brush-covered northeast slope, beaten and afraid.

'What'n hell was all that about?' Coleman asked when Koch and the other cowboys had the restless cattle back under control.

No-one replied. There was no need. The answer was obvious; the Indians had been after their supplies.

While the rest of the crew slowly put the shock of the sudden attack behind them and Kane secured the area, O'Brien started checking on the five bodies littering the ground around the post.

The Indian he'd hammered in the face was the only one still alive. He was thirty or so, and fighting against tears. As O'Brien looked down at him he felt something unpleasant slip through his innards. Besting a man in combat was one thing. But when that man was in no way your equal...

O'Brien started feeling pretty low.

He left the Athabascan where he was and

113

wandered back to the first brave he'd killed. This one, too, had been an inexperienced fighter, judging by the way he'd held his Walker Colt.

With his mouth narrowing down, O'Brien bent to retrieve the dead man's handgun. He checked it quickly and found it empty. Sniffing the barrel, he realised that it hadn't been fired once during the skirmish.

The Athabascan had attacked them with an empty gun, then. But why—

'*O'Brien!*'

His head snapped around as Kane yelled his name, and he came up expecting more trouble, but froze almost as soon as he saw the twenty or so silhouettes sky-lined on the slowly-darkening northeast slope.

There were about half a dozen women and a whole herd of children ranging from babes-in-arms to sad-faced six-year-olds up there. The women were dressed in patched furs and buckskins, the children in worn hand-me-downs. The two surviving warriors—although it was hardly accurate to describe them as such —stood among them with dark heads bowed.

A small, tortured noise escaped O'Brien's lips as he realised that most of them were weeping.

Suddenly everything that had happened here

began to make sense, for the Athabascans were well-known as a tribe of impoverished nomads. No doubt this particular band had been connected in some way with Raven. And when it became known that Raven was going to act as Bruce-Morgan's guide into the Interior, the other men had tried to talk him into helping them steal some food for their starving families.

But Raven—a man of his word, according to the Scotsman—had refused. There was a fight and Raven was murdered. And after that, his clansmen had lain in wait, planning to attack Bruce-Morgan's crew with little more than knives and empty guns.

O'Brien slowly shook his head as he realised the enormity of what he and the others had just done. For in trying to protect the Scotsman's investment, they'd practically *decimated* this band of pathetic, half-starved wanderers.

Ginny must have realised the same thing, because O'Brien heard her say, 'Oh my God.'

O'Brien came back over to his horse and made a show of slipping his Winchester back into its sheath. Then he coughed away the lump in his throat and called down the line, 'Ed! Cut a decent-sized bull out of the herd, will you?'

Young Harper yelled back, 'Sure!'

O'Brien felt the Scotsman's eyes on him.

115

'Just what do you think you're playing at, O'Brien?'

O'Brien looked up and met Bruce-Morgan's angry gaze. 'I—'

'He's trying to make amends,' Ginny said sharply, annoyed that her brother should even need to ask.

'But... but a *bull!* My God, do you realise that one of those creatures will fetch two thousand dollars by the time we reach—'

O'Brien reached up and grabbed Bruce-Morgan's left wrist. He squeezed hard, until he felt the bones rubbing together. 'Don't *you* realise what we've done to these people?' he asked through clenched teeth. 'Or how desperate they must've been to even *consider* taking us in the first place?' He held the Scotsman's stare until Bruce-Morgan looked away. 'You're damn' right we're gonna make amends. Sam! Let's have a sack of flour out here as well, and some rice and bacon and tea while you're at it.'

Bruce Morgan opened his mouth to protest, but before he could say anything, Ginny said, 'There's some Leibig's extract of beef they might care for, and some deviled ham, too.'

O'Brien nodded gratefully; 'See that they get it, will you?' His eyes turned back to the coppery, tear-streaked faces of the Indians.

116

'What's their language?' he asked quietly.

Kane said, 'Navajo or Apache, I think. Maybe some Chinook.'

'Anyone here speak those tongues?' There was a chorus of negatives. 'Damn.'

'Why?' asked Kane.

O'Brien met his gaze with sad eyes. 'It probably wouldn't count for much now,' he replied. 'But I just wanted to tell 'em that I'm sorry.'

After they made their offerings to the Athabascans and watched them collect their dead and leave, O'Brien busied himself getting Bruce-Morgan's small band settled into Stotter's Post for the night. The cowboys got the herd shifted off the trail and Ringgold patched up the windows and helped fix Ginny's Sibley tent outside while Coleman cooked up some eats and O'Brien dragged Raven out back and dug a shallow grave in the damp soil.

Much later, once the wind picked up and blew around the cabin, they ate. Of them all, only Kane had any real appetite. The rest chewed and swallowed simply because to go hungry meant lowering their resistance to the growing cold.

Afterwards, O'Brien took first watch. He was glad to grab some time to himself. Huddled in his sheepskin jacket with his rifle in easy reach, he looked out across the tundra and thought about the widows he and the others had made today.

The wagons had been stalled side by side near the trading post's west-facing wall, and a rope corral had been strung close by to contain the horses. About fifty yards due north, the cattle grazed and bellowed, sounding lonely in the night.

O'Brien had been alone for about twenty minutes when he heard a cabin door open and close behind him. He turned to the sound of footsteps and saw Ginny silvered by the faint moon-glow, a mug of coffee clasped in her hands. The appetising aroma of hot Arbuckle was whipped this way and that by the chilly norther.

'Here,' she said. 'I imagine you could use this.'

He smiled his thanks and took the mug, but instead of returning to the relative warmth of the cabin, she stayed where she was. 'Snow tonight,' she remarked with an air of authority. 'I've seen clouds like these before, in the Yukon Territory, and they always presage a heavy fall.'

O'Brien tried the coffee, then asked, 'Has your brother decided what he's going to do now that we haven't got anyone to guide us to the gold-fields?' It was easier for him to find out what was going on through the girl rather than wait for Bruce-Morgan to tell him, because the atmosphere between them had been decidedly frosty ever since their run-in over O'Brien's treatment of the beaten Athabascans.

'We'll go on alone,' she replied. 'After all, we've got a map—of sorts—and a degree of common sense. And with any luck we ought to find another guide at the first Tlingit camp we come to.'

He took another sip of coffee. 'If you're sure.'

'We're sure,' she said. 'You know...' Her tone turned awkward, almost embarrassed. 'This isn't very easy for me to say, O'Brien, but...'

'Yes'm?'

She hugged herself against the cold, secretly glad that his attention was still on their surroundings and not on her. 'I misjudged you,' she said at last. 'When we first met, I mean. I looked at you and saw just another man with a gun. But I was wrong.'

'What makes you think that?' he asked cynically.

She considered before answering. 'The loyalty you've displayed since we started out on this trek. Your compassion for those poor Indians.' He turned to look down at her, surprised by her words, and this time she was glad, because she wanted him to see her sincerity. 'I've known a lot of men in my time, O'Brien, and there's not one of them who didn't put himself before everyone else. But you... you're different. You fight and you kill, yes—and yet you also *care*.'

She forced a laugh to stop things getting too serious. 'It's not often that a man makes me feel good to be a woman. But you do. When I look at you, I think that maybe I'm wrong. Maybe there *are* a few decent men left in this world.'

Carefully he said, 'That sounds to me like you once got burned by a bad one.'

'I did,' she replied softly. There was a moment of awkward silence as she looked up into his face. 'Anyway,' she said at length. 'I... I just wanted you to know how I felt.'

'I appreciate it, ma'am,' he said, meaning it.

He watched her disappear into the darkness just as the first drifting snowflakes began to pepper the night air.

A day and a half later the bad weather had even stretched as far as the Gulf, and Yacutat lay beneath a thin but steadily-growing mantle of snow.

In their crude log cabins, the town's inhabitants tried to sit the blizzard out in as much comfort as possible. Few people ventured out onto the streets; there wasn't any need.

That was why the *Pamela Royal* strained and wheezed into port unannounced, her funereal black bulk rising like some biblical leviathan through the shifting, all-but-impenetrable wall of wind-blown snow.

One of her funnels was missing. Her deck was scorched and charred. Weird, unhealthy clanking sounds came from her boiler-room and her prow was shattered almost beyond repair.

Two men stood on her foredeck, braving the storm. Both of them were well-wrapped against the blowing gale. One was taller than the other, with shifty green eyes and a smile just left of centre. His companion was shorter, with bowed legs and the build of a pit bull.

Their names were Harvey Goodlight and J P Riley.

And in their eyes was the burning light of vengeance.

SIX

Bruce-Morgan's party continued trending north across the ponderous uplands, their progress hampered considerably by the savage weather.

Above them the sky retained its leaden quality. Snow continued to fall in a swirling, silvery screen. The land—largely featureless to begin with—lay like an endless white blanket on all sides.

For two days they'd struggled against the elements, O'Brien out front, his quarter-horse stepping high through the foot-deep snow; the Conestogas rattling and swaying along behind; the Herefords bawling complaints; Kane bringing up the rear with his mule in tow, holding his *grulla* on a tight rein lest it slip in the cattle's slushy back-trail.

And then, just when the snow began to show signs of abating, the wind blew up afresh, blasting the first stinging needles of a new fall into their exposed faces.

Their already cautious pace slowed to a crawl, and O'Brien saw little to be gained by trying to battle on. He spotted a stand of coniferous trees that looked as if they might provide a decent wind-break about two hundred yards away and reined in, waiting for Bruce-Morgan to catch him up.

Shouting to make himself heard, he told the Scotsman that he thought they should call it a day.

'But it's only a little past noon!' Bruce-Morgan protested.

'I'm only telling you what I think,' O'Brien called back.

With difficulty the Scotsman turned in the saddle. He was bundled up in a heavy, shin-length coat of buffalo skin and his hat was tied to his head with a thick woollen scarf. Behind them the rest of the column trailed woefully across the pristine snow-field, their progress awkward and stumbling, made in a series of jerky stops and starts.

'You're probably right,' he conceded after a moment. 'All right, O'Brien, lead us to that timber and I'll pass word back.'

It took them the better part of another hour to reach the trees and prepare camp. By the time they were through, the animals had been quartered beneath the relative shelter of the spruce and Ginny's tent had been erected between the wagons.

Coleman's first job was to get a wind-whipped fire going and shovel snow into a pot in order to fix coffee. When he also suggested cooking up a pan of pea-soup, those closest to him showed their enthusiasm by telling him to quit talking and get on with it.

Surveying their surroundings a few yards away, O'Brien was pleased to see that he had chosen their campsite well. Although the ground was hilly, there was enough flat land to afford them a comfortable enough bivouac until the weather allowed them to move on once again. Likewise, although there was plenty of forage for their animals, he had no reason to believe that they had encroached upon a game-trail and might later find themselves having to deal with an irate grizzly.

Listening to the moaning of the wind, he shivered. If he'd had any sense he'd have gone south for the winter, not north. Still, it was a bit late for wishful thinking now, and it was as well to make the best of things the way they were. According to Bruce-Morgan, another thirty north-bound miles should bring them to a Tlingit encampment. Their progress might get easier then, once the supplies were re-packed aboard sleds.

Hearing someone crunching through the snow behind him, he turned and saw Tom

Koch approaching as fast as the gusty weather would allow. The cowboy's usually-pale face was now ruddy with the cold, and his heavy breathing was marked by thick clouds of vapour.

He looked worried.

'What's up?' O'Brien asked when the younger man was near enough.

'Ed Harper,' Koch replied. 'He looks awful poorly, Mr O'Brien. Miss Ginny's takin' a look at him, but she's not sure what it is that's ailin' him. C'd *you* come an' take a look?'

O'Brien didn't waste breath on words. He used one gloved hand to gesture back the way Koch had come and together they retraced their steps to the centre of the camp, where Coleman was fixing his stew and a few of the others were bending over Harper's prone form.

'What happened?' O'Brien asked as they slipped and slid across to the young red-head.

'Well,' the Bible-reader replied, 'he was loose in the bowels this mornin', quiet too. Then he perked up a little. But when he off-saddled his cayuse just now he went pale as a ghost. Couple minutes later he threw up.'

Just then they reached the sick boy. Around him were crowded Bruce-Morgan, Ringgold, Hermanas and Brand. Ginny was kneeling beside the patient; his face was flushed and there was a sickly smell about him that spoke of still more diarrhoea.

O'Brien knelt opposite the girl and said, 'What do you make of it?'

She shook her head, her own lips pale and her dark eyes concerned. 'I'm not sure. But he's got a fever, I can tell you that much. The poor wretch is burning up.'

O'Brien frowned. Until he heard that he'd half-decided that Harper was suffering from some kind of food poisoning. Sharper than intended, he glanced up at the expectant faces surrounding them and said, 'Move back, will you, and give the poor feller some air. You too, Ginny.'

What he really meant was: *Keep your distance until we know he's not contagious.*

He scanned Harper's face closely. The skin was so red that his freckles had disappeared into the feverish hue. As he looked down at the boy, the boy opened his eyes and returned his stare. Harper's eyes were glassy and they kept shifting in and out of focus.

'Sorry...' Harper husked weakly. 'To be a burden, I mean.'

'Forget it,' O'Brien replied gently. He glanced down at the boy's gloved hands, which were folded across his narrow chest in the kind of way a corpse is usually laid out. Willing himself not to hesitate and spook the others, he reached down and peeled one of the boy's gloves off.

Harper's hands had long, work-roughened fingers.

They were also very blotchy.

O'Brien muttered, *'Damn.'*

'What is it?' Ringgold asked nervously.

Instead of answering the question, O'Brien addressed one of his own to the sick young cowboy. 'Ed—have you drunk from any of the pools or streams we've passed in the last day or so? Ed?'

The boy stirred, coming back out of his doze. 'Drunk...? No sir. No, wait yeah. Yeah, I filled my canteen when we spelled th'horses at the river bar yest'day noon.'

O'Brien's shoulders slumped with the depth of his sigh. 'All right, boy,' he said calmly. 'Listen to me. Unless I'm mistaken, you've got beaver fever—'

'Huh?' It was Ringgold.

'—but don't fret. It's nothing we can't fix. Just lie still a while and try to get some sleep. We'll take care of everything.'

Harper nodded sluggishly. 'Yes sir.'

O'Brien glanced up into Ginny's eyes. 'Blankets,' he said tersely. 'As many as you can rustle up. We're gonna have to sweat it out of him.'

'Here, you c'n have mine,' Hermanas said without hesitation.

'Mine too,' said Brand.

'Thanks. And someone fetch me a canteen of *boiled* water. We've got to make sure we replace whatever fluid this boy loses when he *really* starts to sweat.'

Before anyone could move, however, Harper began shivering, cold inside despite the fever. His teeth clacked together with such force that O'Brien thought they might shatter, and as the boy's tremblings grew stronger the freelance fighting man took a grip on his biceps and held him down.

'Hurry up with those blankets, will you?' he snapped over one shoulder.

Sweat popped on the youngster's forehead and trickled slowly across his burning skin in a series of salty snail-trails. Another noisome stench came up as he lost control of his bowels. Ignoring it, O'Brien continued to hold him down until finally the tremors passed and the boy lay spent.

'Sir?' Harper croaked in a low voice, so that the others, who'd gone off to carry out O'Brien's orders, wouldn't hear him.

'Yes, boy?'

'Am I gonna die?'

O'Brien reached down to put a reassuring

hand on his shoulder. 'Not if I've got anything to do with it,' he replied.

But if the truth be told, he just didn't know for sure.

Back in Yacutat, Harvey Goodlight got the ten hardcases still left on his payroll kitted out with thick, hard-wearing coats and boots, then waited impatiently down at the town's only tavern for the weather to clear.

The entrepreneur from Port Angeles was still smarting from the outcome of their run-in with the *Vancouver Belle*. Four men dead, another two wounded, and the steamer—one of two he co-owned, which usually ran cargo up and down the west coast—virtually destroyed.

Not to put too fine a point on it, he was feeling royally pissed-off.

Pretty much the same could also be said of J P Riley. But now the stocky little gunman with the broken nose and habit of humming all the time was more eager to catch up with O'Brien and settle a score for what had happened in the Missoula dentist's surgery than anything else.

It was only by luck that Goodlight had been able to straighten things out with one of the sheriff's deputies before the whole thing went to court. A cockamamie story about mix-ups

129

and misunderstandings, plus a dozen or more apologies, had finally secured his release. That, and a fifty-dollar 'consideration' to the dentist.

Now Riley wanted O'Brien's ears.

But in his own way, Riley too was a professional. He'd spent many a year selling his gun, and as much as he ached for revenge, he also knew the value of caution. Besides which, the rest of the men, no doubt still shaken by the catastrophic turnaround in their attempt at piracy, didn't appear too keen to lock horns with the Scotsman's party again.

Riley said as much to Goodlight as they sat sharing a corner table across the room from the others, but to his surprise Goodlight did not appear overly annoyed.

'Once bitten, twice shy, eh?' he remarked absently over a mug of steaming coffee. 'Still, I'd have expected better of them, J P. I mean, just look at them. There isn't one who'd look out of place down on the Barbary Coast.'

'Oh, they're tough enough,' Riley said, feeling that he should say something in their defence, especially since it was he who had hired them in the first place. 'They're killers all. But...' He paused, dropping his already quiet voice even lower. 'Let's just say they like the odds on *their* side when they go into action.'

Goodlight looked directly into the black eyes

lurking beneath Riley's heavy brows and smiled a smile to match the weather. 'In that case,' he said smoothly, 'we'll have to make sure they have the odds stacked just the way they like them. In fact...' He eyed the hardcases sidelong. 'In *fact*, J P—I've just had an idea by which we can take over every single piece of that blasted Scotsman's merchandise without even firing a shot. And I think your so-called "Killers" will find it exactly to their taste.'

When O'Brien was sure the boy would come to no more harm, he swallowed hard, straightened up and went across to the others. 'Anybody else here drunk stream or river water since we set foot in Alaska?' he demanded urgently.

Relief washed through him as the others shook their heads. 'Only in coffee,' said Coleman.

'That's all right. As long as it's boiled it's okay. But from now on, watch yourselves. First sign of trouble—spewing up or getting the runs like Harper there, come tell me.'

'You bet,' said Ringgold.

'Mr O'Brien?' asked Koch.

O'Brien met his gaze. He looked scared. 'What?'

'Is Ed gonna die?'

The freelance fighting man dropped his eyes. 'Tom,' he began, pausing when he felt his chest tighten with emotion. 'I'm almighty sorry to tell you that he just did.'

There was a moment of stunned silence. Then Ginny paused midway through gathering blankets and shook her head, plainly horrified.

'No,' she whispered. Then, louder; *'No!'*

To confirm what he'd just said O'Brien nodded, not trusting himself to speak straightaway. Then he said, 'Before you all start asking questions, I'd better tell you—I've got no answers. I've never known beaver fever to kill a man. Leastways not kill him so quick. Hell, maybe it wasn't beaver fever at all. Maybe it was something else in the water. I just don't know.' He grabbed up one of the blankets, turned on his heel and stalked over to the body, covering it reverently and then staring off into the snowy distance.

Behind him, Ginny put back the rest of the blankets, too stunned for tears. The pea-soup began to burn but nobody moved to lift the pan from the flames. 'Ed... *gone?*' Koch muttered in disbelief. Almost angrily he wiped away the tears spilling from his one good eye before they could freeze.

Kane got a shovel, walked off a few dozen

feet and started digging.

Thirty minutes later Ed was ready for burying. They gathered around the recently-dug trench, lowered the blanket-wrapped body into the hole and filled it in while Bruce-Morgan read the Twenty-Third Psalm.

It was a solemn and moving movement. O'Brien knew it would stay with him forever.

That evening the blizzard which had started at noon finally blew itself out, leaving the open plains strangely calm and silent. An opening appeared in the clouds and a shaft of moonlight slanted down from the heavens to illuminate the smooth, snow-draped steppes.

Not a thing moved.

'Thank God that's behind us,' Bruce-Morgan said after a while, breaking the almost preternatural hush.

One by one the small band began to stir, climbing from out of their soogans to ease their cramped muscles. Coleman found a stick and poked their campfire back to life, and soon the coffee-pot was bubbling merrily, but the storm had gone on for so long that now they found themselves temporarily hard of hearing.

The breeze was still sharp, but not as cutting as it had been just a few moments before. Standing beside O'Brien, Ginny watched it drive the still-weighty snowclouds further south, then made a small sound of wonder when the dark sky began to shimmer and oscillate to an ever-shifting pattern of colours snaking up from the northern horizon.

'God A'mighty!' Coleman muttered.

'*Jesucristo,*' whispered Hermanas, crossing himself.

'Don't panic,' Bruce-Morgan said quickly. 'It's only the *aurora borealis.*'

'The whore's *what?*' asked Coleman.

'The *aurora borealis,*' Bruce-Morgan repeated. 'Maybe you'd know it better as the Northern Lights.'

'My God,' said Koch. 'It's beautiful.'

The others shared his view, each of them awe-struck by the natural, but somehow *more* than natural, phenomenon.

'Sure wish Ed could've seen it,' muttered Jack Brand.

He spoke for them all.

Some time later they bedded down. After a while sleep claimed all but those on guard or nighthawk duty. At sun-up next morning they moved out again—but not before each of them had paid his last, silent respects to Ed Harper, whose grave was now marked only by an oblong of small, misshapen rocks.

Again their progress was slow, until O'Brien

suggested that the Herefords be herded up ahead to flatten out an easier trail for the wagons to follow. That speeded things up a bit, but their pace still remained torturous.

Now a new chain of mountains shelved into sight about five or six hundred yards ahead, its jagged peaks hazy with low-lying cloud. 'Are you sure there's a way over that range?' O'Brien asked sceptically.

'Yes,' Bruce-Morgan replied quietly. Although each of them had been shaken by Harper's death, the Scotsman had taken it worst of all, no doubt feeling a special responsibility to the men in his employ. He was still subdued.

As the sun climbed slowly higher and then began its westering descent, they crossed a vast, and hitherto unblemished, field of snow and began to ascend even deeper into the eerily quiet foothills, the cattle ploughing an ungainly but nonetheless serviceable track through which the Conestogas could rumble and slide.

The way Bruce-Morgan told it, he'd travelled through these parts once before, about six months earlier, on Hudson's Bay Company business. But six months ago the timbered hills rising to either side of them hadn't been covered in a concealing sheet of snow, and now everything looked the same, no matter which

135

way the Scotsman glanced.

Two hours into the climb he finally confessed to being hopelessly lost.

O'Brien had already guessed as much but bore him no malice. 'Well,' he consoled laconically, studying the clear blue sky, 'at least we're still heading north.'

He reined in and dismounted, passing the reins up to Bruce-Morgan. 'Spell the animals!' he called back down the line.

The column came to a halt in a winding channel about sixty feet wide and a quarter of a mile long. The slopes stretching gently away to either side were a mixture of pale blue and pure white, broken only by a few stunted trees and bushes and the tracks of wolves, red foxes, ground squirrels and marmots.

But it was the glare caused by the sun bouncing off the eastern slope that drew O'Brien's attention most of all. For the first time since they'd started out he found himself considering the dangers of snow-blindness.

Bending, he scraped away a foot or more of snow until he came to a sickly green splash of tussock grass. Then he tore at the frozen topsoil until he reached the loose, damp earth beneath. Without ceremony he smeared his cheeks with dirt, leaving two wide brown bands beneath his eyes.

Realising what he was doing and seeing the wisdom of it, the Scotsman also dismounted and smeared his face in similar fashion, telling the others to follow suit. 'The dirt'll keep the snow-glare from bouncing off your cheeks and into your eyes,' he explained.

'Does that include *me?*' Kane asked drily.

Bruce-Morgan looked into the black man's face and they shared a good-natured grin. 'No, not you, Ches. You're excused.'

For a time the winding mountain channel was quiet as the rest of the men did as they were told. Then O'Brien scanned their surroundings once more.

'As long as we keep going north we should be all right,' he said at length, thinking aloud more than anything else. 'All right. Mount up, everybody! First thing's to get out of this groove and onto the flat land. And after that...' he pulled his Stetson lower onto his head. 'After that we make camp and start out afresh in the morning.'

'Yo!' cried Kane.

The column slowly got back under way— this time apparently manned by a chorus of Mississippi minstrels.

Before sunrise the following morning, Kane took it upon himself to go out ahead and see

137

if he could scare up a likely-looking trail. Within forty-five minutes he was back.

'I think I had me a little luck,' he announced, taking a plate of bacon and beans from Coleman and hunkering beside the campfire. 'They's a lake up ahead, surrounded by timber. Water's all but froze over now, but I discerned a track swingin' to the north an' east that 'pears to cut a natural course through these hills.'

'Good work,' said Bruce-Morgan, scratching at his own bristly chin. 'All right, men, you heard what Chester just said. We'll move out in fifteen minutes!'

It took them most of the day to follow the twisting mountain trail, again in a series of stops and starts as problems cropped up and took time to overcome. But by four o'clock, with the sky already darkening and what Coleman called 'the whore that bore Alice' flashing across the firmament, they reached the foothills of the far side and found a decent wind-break beside which to make camp for the night.

Next morning they were back on fairly level ground, forging a new trail through ice-crusted snowdrifts two or three feet deep, O'Brien still watchful even though the land surrounding them seemed devoid of life.

Two days out of the mountains they reached

the Tlingit camp Bruce-Morgan had mentioned.

The place had been constucted on a grass-
and timber-rich plateau not far from a salmon-
heavy tributary that meandered north in a series
of quirky bends, and even had they not been
starved of civilisation they would have found
the commune impressive.

To his suprise, O'Brien discovered that the
Tlingits—of which he estimated there to be
a few hundred occupying this stretch of the
Interior—lived in stoutly-built wood cabins.

In appearance their flat, moon-shaped faces
favoured those of their more northern cousins,
the Eskimos. They all appeared well-dressed,
wore their thick black hair to shoulder-length
and viewed the newcomers' arrival with much
curiosity.

They were just about as different from the
unfortunate Athabascans as they could get,
O'Brien thought dismally. In their time they'd
been bloodthirsty warriors who were slow to
trust the white man. They'd kept captives as
slaves and worshipped a whole assortment of
animal and bird gods, as evidenced by the long
row of intricately carved totem-poles reaching
fifty feet skyward along the plateau's southwest
ridge.

And yet perversely, they were also among the

most civilised of tribes. Sturdy wooden fishing-boats had been beached along the water's edge, and the camp's livestock, which consisted mainly of grey, wire-haired dogs, were penned away neatly in babiche corrals.

The whole area was filled with dogs' barking, the chatter of women and laughter of children. The plateau smelled of fish and woodsmoke and bear grease, but to O'Brien and the others it represented life in an otherwise sterile wilderness.

As Hermanas, Koch and Brand yipped and whistled the Herefords up the slope and off the trail, a few dozen parka-clad Indians shushed toward them in webbed snowshoes. The men carried lances and bows, but did not appear overly hostile. Indeed, several of them appeared to recognise Bruce-Morgan, and cracked broad smiles in his direction.

The wagons ground to a halt and Ginny dropped down to the snowy earth, hurrying toward the head of the column just as a large man in a voluminous coat of otter pelts pushed through the copper-faced throng to greet them.

'Bru-mo!' he said, grasping the Scotsman by one hand. 'You come back.' He peered around. 'And bring sister, too!'

Still astride his horse, O'Brien studied what

he assumed to be the village headman. He was about sixty years of age, with silver streaks running the length of his otherwise dark hair. Like the rest of his people, his bronzed face was creased and weathered by the harsh elements, his cheeks round and high, his eyes black and outwardly cordial. Aside from his size (few of the Tlingits appeared to grow much above five and a half feet), the only thing that set him apart from the rest of them were the *pince-nez* perched comically on the end of his round, blackhead-dotted nose.

As if sensing O'Brien's eyes on him, the headman twisted his own rugged countenance up to return the scrutiny. 'I am Konnig,' he said after a moment, obviously very proud of the name.

O'Brien nodded a greeting. 'And I am O'Brien,' he replied, matching the Tlingit's formality.

'Welcome, O'Brien,' Konnig said with a small bow. 'Welcome to *all* who claim friendship with our ally, Bru-mo!'

SEVEN

Konnig's English was good, but not so good that he could easily pronounce Bruce-Morgan's name. That was why he'd shortened it to 'Bru-mo'.

Still, the Scotsman was obviously something of a celebrity among the Indians, and curious, O'Brien asked Ginny why.

It turned out that the *tyone*, or chief—who was half-Tlingit, half-Haida—had first met her brother about three years before, at a time when his tribe was in serious danger of being wiped out by a smallpox epidemic. Evidently Bruce-Morgan had packed much-needed medicine out to the beleaguered people and saved them from extinction. Not surprisingly, they now considered him to be a great hero.

They even decided to honour his presence with one of the lavish banquets for which they were famous. The affair was held in the largest clan-house—Konnig's, naturally—and there was much music and dancing and eating. The food included salmon, seal and caribou meat, delicately-prepared birds and their eggs, berries, roots and even wild greens. Steaming tea washed the delicacies down; alcohol—already the ruin of their brothers down along Alaska's southeast coast—was not permitted.

It was during the festivities that Bruce-Morgan and Konnig made arrangements to transport the supplies from here to the goldfields by sled. The chief also cheerfully agreed to look after the Conestogas until the Scotsman returned, asking only a nominal payment of some cattle and sweetmeats in return for use of his men.

'But Bru-mo stay with us a while before moving on, yes?' Konnig asked.

'Of course. I'm never anxious to leave the hospitality of Konnig's Tlingits,' Bruce-Morgan replied in the somewhat starched and ceremonial way the Indians favoured. 'I thought we might stay a couple of days before setting out again, if you'll have us.'

Konnig chuckled and slapped him on the back. 'That is good!' he enthused. 'But enough talk of business and leaving, Bru-mo. You've only just arrived! Come, eat! You've hardly touched that grass-stuffed grebe!'

Around mid-morning next day O'Brien was trimming his whiskers in the cabin Konnig had offered his guests for the duration of their stay when he heard some kind of commotion out-side. Jack Brand, who was nearest the shaved-ice window, went over to find out what was going on.

'Looks like ole Konnig's got visitors,' he said after a moment.

'Visitors?'

O'Brien and the cabin's other occupants—Ringgold, Koch and Hermanas—crossed the spartan room to see for themselves. Beyond the crude but effective window they spotted two fur-clad newcomers mushing virtually empty sleds up the incline and onto the plateau, crack-ing whips above the heads of their straining, five-dog teams.

'White men?' Ringgold enquired.

'Could be,' muttered Brand. But it was dif-ficult to tell. The faces of both men were hid-den behind thick scarves, and beaver-pelt hats were jammed low over their foreheads.

Following O'Brien's lead, the others grabb-ed their own heavy jackets and buttoned up against the cold. By the time they filed out into the fairly flat square of ground bordered by the larger clan-houses, most of the Indians were trotting forward to confront the new arrivals themselves.

The day hadn't brightened much beyond the first grey light of cock-crow, and odd, moderate

144

snow-showers had been falling off and on ever since midnight. But as the freelance fighting man and his companions joined the throng, there was enough light to confirm that the visitors were indeed white.

They yelled for their teams to slow and stop, which they duly did, stalling the sleds in the middle of the camp's cleared central area, then released their grips on the handrails and reach-ed up to yank down their scarves.

Both men were in their late thirties, with nar-row, squinting eyes and thick, ice-encrusted beards. The first had a creased copper face and a large, lumpy nose. His partner was a shade taller, with a more sallow complexion and slighter build. White vapour dribbled from their nostrils as they returned the Tlingits' curious stares with just a trace of arrogance.

'You got a headman around here?' asked the first man, rubbing his gloved hands together. The way he pronounced each word implied that he was talking to imbeciles. 'Unnerstand me? Speak-ee English?'

As he had done the previous day, Konnig pushed through the crowd with his head held high and the weak sunlight spilling off his *pince-nez*. Behind him came Bruce-Morgan and Ginny, who had been invited to share the chief's clan-house until they left.

145

The two newcomers were obviously surprised to see white people among the sea of round, burnished faces on all sides. Glancing deeper into the crowd, they spotted O'Brien and the others; Kane and Coleman, too.

'Well lookee here!' muttered the second man. 'How-do, mister, ma'am! Sure never reckoned on finding no civilised folk up here!'

Konnig came to a halt before them, his own generous height dwarfing them. He studied them soberly for a moment, and O'Brien could tell by the set of his mouth that he didn't much care for what he saw.

'I am Konnig,' he said. 'You have business here?'

'Sure do,' said the first man. He stuck out his right hand. 'The name's Jones, Dick Jones, late of the Susitna River country. This here's my partner, Gene Curry. Good to meet you Konnig.' When the chief made no move to take the proffered hand, Jones turned his brown eyes to Bruce-Morgan, who then stepped forward and introduced both himself and his sister.

'You have business here?' Konnig intoned again.

The affability Jones had displayed just a few moments before seemed to evaporate under the chief's unblinking stare. Watching from his

146

place among the crowd, O'Brien saw the fellow struggle mightily to keep his smile in place.

'Hell yes, iffen you'll pardon my French, ma'am,' Jones replied with a wink at Ginny. 'Like I jus' told you, me'n Gene here are up from the Susitna River. Been pannin' for colour thereabouts with middlin' success. But thing's been a touch rough jus' lately, what with this dang-blasted weather an' all, so we decided to quit and go winter up at Arnesen's place over to Suslota Pass.'

Konnig stood in silence, waiting for the other man to continue.

'Well,' Dick Jones went on, 'let me tell you, things at Arnesen's is in a pretty sorry state. That Norwegian's barely got enough grub to keep his own belly full, let alone takin' in boarders too. So we figured to come down here an' mebbe trade some gee-gaws for a little sustenance.'

Konnig stared off across the snow-patched plateau, the eyes behind his comical glasses thoughtful. On the surface, the white man's request seemed fair enough. But with one or two exceptions, experience had taught him that most whites had a nasty habit of speaking around corners.

'We can give you some food,' he decided at last. 'Some fish and caribou meat. Enough to see you on your way. We do not seek payment. Just take it and go.'

Jones dipped his shaggy head gratefully. 'Thank you right kindly, Konnig. You got a real generous spirit. But we was kinda hopin' you'd spare us a little *more'n* that. See, me an' Gene here, we was figurin' to take somethin' back to Arnesen's with us, mebbe re-sell it to a few o' the fellers campin' up in the Pass.'

Konnig shook his head. 'That is not possible,' he said.

'Oh, we c'n pay,' the bearded sourdough cut in quickly, rummaging in the small canvas-wrapped bundle tied to his sled. 'Here, look. You like knives? We got plenty knives. Beads for yore wimmin? Bright, shiny mirrors—'

Konnig raised a calloused palm to silence him. 'We do not have so much food that we could affort to barter it,' he said.

Jones' face assumed a new, sullen look, and his brown eyes gave out a dangerous, warning flare. 'That's what *you* say,' he spat. 'But what about all them cattle yonder? You c'd afford to trade a couple beeves, couldn't you?'

'The cattle are not mine to trade,' the Tlingit chief replied, unruffled by the other man's outburst.

'Well, if they ain't yours—'

'They belong to *me*,' Bruce-Morgan interrupted, stepping forward. 'And if you're considering buying for resale to your friends up in Suslota Pass, I'm sure I could quote you an acceptable price.'

The already-narrowed eyes of Jones and Curry slitted down even more. 'What kinda price?' Curry asked in a low voice.

The Scotsman glanced over toward the milling herd, doing a few mental calculations. Then he returned his ruddy, square face to the sourdoughs and smiled. 'Fifteen hundred dollars,' he said.

'*What?*'

'Are you outta yore brain, mister? Fifteen hunnerd fer a *cow?*'

Ginny came up to stand alongside her brother, eyeing the newcomers levelly. 'To men starved of beef,' she explained, 'men we know for a *fact* to be sluicing four or five hundred dollars out of their claims every month, I should say it's cheap at half the price.'

'An' half the price is what I'm offerin',' Jones replied, scratching some ice from his heavy moustache. 'A mite *less'n* half, to be accurate. Five hundred dollars, tops.'

'My dear sir,' Bruce-Morgan said, smiling. 'You know as well as I that a prime Hereford cow will fetch around two thousand dollars out here.'

149

Jones dropped his gaze. He knew it, all right. 'Take it or leave it,' he replied brusquely. 'It's too dang cold fer dickerin'. Five hundred dollars fer one o' them cows. An' I'll make you a decent price on anythin' else you got fer sale.'

The Sotsman studied him shrewdly, while around them the gathered Indians and whites watched on. Then Bruce-Morgan shook his head sadly. 'I'm sorry,' he said firmly but politely. 'I don't believe we can do business. Oh, I'll quote you prices on anything you like, certainly, prices which will enable you to resell at a handsome profit. But I will not *give* my stock away, sir. It's cost us too much already— and not just financially.'

Jones and Curry exchanged a look. Were it not for the fact that they were surrounded by the Scotsman's allies, they might well have considered indulging in a little larceny. As it was, however, Jones only turned his weathered eyes back to the Scot and assumed a look of profound regret.

'I am purely sorry to hear you say that, Mr Bruce-Morgan,' he replied. 'Because I don't b'lieve you'll get a better offer anyplace else out here. Not in Suslota Pass, not on the Susitna River nor Forty Mile, either.'

'We'll take our chances,' the Scotsman

replied coolly.

The wind picked up around them, harsh and piercing.

'My offer stands,' Konnig said into the silence. 'You may take food enough for yourselves before—'

'Shove your food!' Jones snarled angrily.

Although few of the Tlingits understood English, all of them understood tones, and Jones' was decidedly unfriendly. A low muttering went through the Indians surrounding them, but Konnig barked a few words in Chinook that quietened them down.

'Go,' he advised the sourdoughs.

Curry hawked up a wad of phlegm and spat it at Bruce-Morgan's feet. 'Don't fret,' he replied. 'We're goin'.'

But they'll be back, O'Brien thought. There was no mistaking the greed in their eyes. He watched them return to their sleds and take hold of the handrails, and thought again. *They'll be back.*

As sure as guns are iron.

He was right, too. They *did* come back. At two-thirty next morning.

A wind-whipped blizzard had blown up around midnight, draping a fresh white blanket across the land. Jones and Curry sat out the

151

first ninety minutes in a stand of timber about two miles to the south, huddled around a small fire and cradling mugs of Arbuckle until Jones judged the time to be right.

'Now sh'd do it,' he pronounced at last. It was around one-thirty a.m.

'Are you sure?' Curry asked, hesitating. 'I mean—'

'We're never gonna get a better chance,' Jones cut in irritably. 'Who in hell would ever expect trouble on a night like this?' He threw the remains of his coffee into the fire and watched a cloud of grey smoke rise up and be torn apart by the bitter wind. ' 'Sides, you saw them there wagons as well as me. Looked pretty loaded down, the pair of 'em.'

'Yeah,' Curry allowed, avarice replacing doubt in his tone. 'Loaded down with all manner of foodstuffs, I'll bet.'

'Come on, then. By the time we get back to that camp, the Scotchman an' his Indian buddies'll be well settled in for the night. We can take as much as we can from the wagons and be long gone afore anyone wakes up enough to notice.'

With Jones taking the lead, they took up their positions behind their sleds and mushed their teams north out of the timber and into the teeth of the blizzard. Visibility was poor,

152

to say the least, but the men had learned months before to trust the instincts of their dogs. Even so, the journey was not without its dangers. About half-way back to the plateau Curry lost control of his sledge and the whole rig spilled onto one side. They lost a quarter-hour setting it up again and checking the dogs' lines.

By two-thirty the Tlingit encampment was in sight, a ghost town beneath the spectral, uncertain light of the distant moon. Braking about a hundred yards away, the sourdoughs scanned the snow-piled incline leading up onto the flatland.

As Jones had surmised, Konnig's people rarely posted guard. In this Godforsaken wilderness, and in this kind of weather, there was little need. Every so often the howling of the Indians' corralled dogs could be heard above the moaning of the wind, but that was all.

'Right,' Jones muttered. Tugging down his snow-damp scarf, he turned to his companion. 'We'll leave the sleds here an' go the rest o' the way on foot. Once we've made it to the wagons, we'll help ourselves to as much as we can, toss it down that western slope, then come back here, mush around and pick it up.'

Curry nodded, exaggerating the motion to

make sure that Jones saw it. 'What if we *do* run into a guard or two up there?' he asked. He already knew the answer. They'd discussed it earlier. But he was kind of hoping that Dick might've come up with a new plan by now; one that didn't necessarily involve murder.

He hadn't.

Taking a curl-bladed skinning-knife from a sheath on the belt around his waist, he smiled unpleasantly. 'We send 'em up the Green River,' he responded.

Curry swallowed. 'All right,' he said after a moment. 'I guess we ain't got much choice, given the circumstances.' He drew in a deep, nerve-steadying breath that made him shiver. 'Okay; let's get to it.'

Leaving their sleds where they were, the two men began to churn up snow on their way to the incline, walking with ponderous footsteps because of the snow-shoes attached to their boots. Around them the wind kept gusting and the snow kept swirling. By the time they reached the top of the slope, their weaving tracks showed grey through the ice-blue snow, already filling in again.

Crouching beside a large, lichen-stained boulder, Jones scanned the camp as best he could.

The place was in darkness. No lights showed anywhere. Snow was piled up against cabin doorways, humped over upturned fishing-boats, smooth and deep across the central clearing.

'Follow me,' he hissed to Curry.

Together they ran as best as they were able along the southern perimeter, hugging whatever cover they could. Jones slipped once and Curry careened into him. There was a moment of cursing, then they righted themselves and continued on around the camp. The only eyes that watched them were those carved into the totem-poles.

By the time they reached their destination —Konnig's clan-house, beside which the two Conestogas had been parked—both men were breathing hard from their exertions, and sweating despite the cold. But as they soaked into the deep shadows between the wagons and the clan-house wall they felt elated, because they had made it this far without being challenged.

'What now?' Curry whispered, putting his mouth close to Jones' ear to be heard above the wind's high-low groaning and the straining creak of cabin-timbers.

'Check the area, make sure we've got it to ourselves,' Jones decided. 'Here, stay put I'll see to it.' He shushed along the cabin until he

155

reached the corner, then peered cautiously through the blizard.

Nothing moved.

He was just about to turn and retrace his footsteps when the wind died down long enough for him to hear the sound of a baby crying not far away. Maybe the brat was hungry. Hell, who wasn't in these parts? Smiling, he moved back along the wall, checked the rear of the clan-house, then rejoined Curry.

'All right,' he muttered. 'Coast's clear. Now all we got to do is dig in. I figger airtights is our best bet. They won't crack or shatter when we throw 'em over the side, an' no matter what's inside 'em, Arnesen's bound to pay well over the odds. Agreed?'

Curry nodded. 'Whatever you say.'

'I'll go take me a look, then, see 'xactly what that Scotchman's packin'. You keep watch at yonder corner. First sign o'trouble, holler an' light out.'

'Got it.'

They split up, resembling two hulking grizzlies in their buffalo-hide overcoats. Curry went to the corner, hugging himself against the sub-zero temperature, and Jones began to struggle with the half-frozen bolts holding the tailgate of the first wagon shut.

156

'...come on, damn you...'

The dry creak the hinges made when he let the tailgate down a moment later was lost beneath the soughing of the wind. Awkward because of the thick mittens he wore, he had to struggle for quite a time before he untied the cord holding the canvas awning shut.

When at last he had it open, the weak moonlight revealed all manner of boxes and kegs.

'Powder River an' let 'er rip!' he muttered, grinning.

He was still grinning when the butt of a Winchester 'One In One Thousand' shot out of the wagon's shadows and clobbered him straight in the face.

'*Uh!*'

He stumbled backwards, hands going up to his ruined nose, keeping his balance only because of the weight-spreading snow-shoes on his feet, and hearing the sounds he made and assuming that a crate had slipped through his hands, Curry turned around and said, 'Fer the love'a God, Dick, keep it down, will y—'

The last word died in his throat.

'Oh Judas—'

He'd seen the man hopping down from out of the wagon earlier. Big feller, battered face, blue eyes, straight nose, salt and pepper beard,

157

cauliflowered ears.

Now the sumbitch had them both covered with a rifle.

'Hands away from your sides!' O'Brien snapped, jerking the Winchester a little to add emphasis to the command. 'And be quick about it!'

But while Curry made to comply, Jones was having none of it. Angered not only by having had his nose broken but also by being cheated out of his booty, his blood-slick face twisted into a mask of fury as he yelled, 'The hell you say!'

He came at O'Brien with the Green River skinning knife in his hand, and Curry waited just long enough to see them clash before wheeling around and lighting out.

Or rather, *trying* to light out.

He hadn't gone more than a dozen paces before a female voice off to his left told him to hold it. There was so much authority in its tone that it didn't occur to him to do anything other than obey. Still, he was damned if he'd give up without a fight. Lord knew what fate he could expect from warriors as savage as the Tlingits.

Pivoting, his left hand streaked across his belly to pull his Smith & Wesson American from its cross-draw holster. As he turned he saw the woman—a tall, beautiful-looking brunette in a sheepskin jacket and black pants—standing in the open doorway of the chief's clan-house. Her hair was some mussed, he noticed idly; more'n likely she'd been sleeping fully clothed.

And armed.

Because she too was holding a Winchester.

'Don't!' she said, her voice rising a pitch as she watched him going for the gun.

But Curry *did*.

The S & W was in his hand and coming around in a sharp arc when Ginny shot him. The blast tore through the howling of the wind and the dogs and Curry screamed, spun and hit the ground nursing a shattered shoulder.

Over by the wagons, O'Brien back-stepped to avoid Jones' first sweeping blow. It would have been the easiest thing in the world to blow the sourdough into the hereafter, and maybe he would've if Jones had been brandishing a gun and not a knife.

As it was, O'Brien back-stepped once more, leading Jones forward, until Ginny's rifle-blast and Curry's scream made both of them pause.

Jones muttered, 'Gene?'

Taking advantage of his momentary distraction, O'Brien again lashed out with the Winchester, this time cracking the barrel down on

Dick Jones' knife-arm.

Jones yelped and released the blade. In the moonlight his bloody face looked ghastly. With another cry he pushed himself away from O'Brien and tore a LeMat from the cavalry-style holster around his waist.

O'Brien yelled, *'Don't try it!'*

He dove for the snow just as Jones fired his first shot. Splinters exploded from the cabin wall where he'd just been. He rolled a few feet and came up just as the pilferous sourdough triggered again.

Even as the bullet ploughed harmlessly into the snow at O'Brien's feet, he slapped the long-gun's stock to his cheek and took aim. There was no time for fancy shooting now. Jones was riled up and dangerous, so it was kill or be killed.

O'Brien squeezed the trigger and his bullet hit the sourdough smack in the chest.

The light-fingered sonofabitch fell back into the darkness, stumbled for a moment, then slipped, then screamed—and fell off the edge of the plateau to snap his neck on some rocks fifty feet below.

Slowly O'Brien straightened to his full height as he heard the sound of footsteps rushing up behind him. Turning, he discerned Bruce-

Morgan, Ginny, Kane, Konnig and some of the others crowding into the churned area behind the clan-house.

'O'Brien, are you all right?' Bruce-Morgan demanded anxiously.

'*I* am,' he replied, hooking a thumb over his shoulder. 'He isn't.'

Bruce-Morgan brushed past him to peer over the snowy ledge and into the darkness beyond. 'My God, man, your hunch was right!' he said, turning back. 'They *did* return! You know, to be perfectly frank with you, I had to agree with Chester here; I never thought we'd see either of them ever again. Still, it's a good thing—'

'What happened to the other one?' O'Brien cut in.

'I shot him,' Ginny replied, stepping out of the gloom. She flashed him a wan smile that betrayed her otherwise calm exterior. 'But he'll live. Konnig here will perform some crude surgery on him and send him home in a week or so, won't you, Konnig?'

The chief inclined his head. 'But he will think twice before he steals again, I think,' he said with a bleak smile.

Imagining just how 'crude' Konnig's surgery would be, O'Brien replied grimly, 'I bet he will at that.'

161

Next morning the supplies were taken from the wagons and stacked aboard light but sturdy sleds, then covered with tarpaulins and lashed down tight. As O'Brien watched all the coming and going from the chilly shade of Konnig's clan-house, Bruce-Morgan told him that since each team-dog—malemutes, he called them— was capable of hauling up to a hundred pounds in weight, the sleds could afford to be well-laden.

A short time later they were finally ready to continue their journey, and after saying their farewells to the chief, the Scotsman and his team took up their places in the waiting line.

Then, heeding the commands of their masters to *mush*, or move, the thick-haired dogs, pricked up their already-pointed ears, wagged their curly tails and leaned into the leather traces.

Amidst all the barking and yelling of directions, the sleds took off across the snowy wilderness once again, the cattle following up in a slow-moving, strung-out line behind them.

Progress picked up considerably, despite the initial problems Coleman and Ringgold had in trying to control the malemutes, and gradually they left the plateau to the south—unaware that Harvey Goodlight's crew were now less than a day behind them.

And closing fast.

EIGHT

Up ahead they ran into another blizzard. The following day came more bad weather. Three days out from Konnig's village they started into the foothills of another mountain range.

The snow had struck hard in the high country. In places the drifts were piled thirty feet deep. Pyramid-shaped pine-trees had crashed earthward beneath its weight, and streams had frozen solid. O'Brien saw petrified fish beneath their glass-like surfaces, so perfectly preserved that they might almost have been exhibits in a museum.

About fifteen miles into the echoing hills they found the remains of a cheeckako—a tenderfoot, or newcomer, as Bruce-Morgan had translated the word. It looked as if the poor sonofabitch had had enough of life in the Interior during winter and tried to pack out. When they found him his sled was a wreck, his dogs were just half-buried mounds of fur and he himself was battered, bloody and frozen solid.

'Looks as if he fell from that ledge yonder,'

the Scotsman remarked grimly, pointing to a trail cutting down across the side of a mountain that even a goat would have difficulty in crossing. 'Come on, let's bury the poor wretch and be on our way.'

For their part, Konnig's packers were a good crowd. They worked hard without complaint, were nearly always to be found smiling and took scrupulous care of their dogs—even to the extent of slipping caribou-hide moccasins over their paws whenever rough country loomed ahead.

That night they called a halt in a bowl of land sheltered to the west by trees, the north by rocks and the east by a sheer cliff-face. There was ample space in which to graze the cattle and horses—once the snow was dug away, of course —and the natural fortifications kept off the worst of the wind.

While Coleman and Ringgold set about erecting Ginny's tent, one of the Tlingits—of whom there were eight in all—fixed supper. Ever since leaving the plateau, man and dogs had shared the same diet; dried salmon, bacon and rice. At first it had seemed palatable. Now it was just plain predictable.

As the night wore on, errant snowflakes hissed in the large, sputtering fire and the Indians, as was their custom, began preparing for another early night. O'Brien, Kane and Bruce-Morgan sat beneath the shelter of the trees, watching Koch, Hermanas and Brand rigging up another makeshift tent over by the foot of the cliff wall. In the distance the baying of wolves and the yapping of the malemutes blended as one.

'Well, gentlemen,' the Scotsman declared over his coffee-cup after they'd been sitting there for fifteen minutes or so. 'By my calculations we're almost there. We should reach Forty Mile in about three or four days from now.'

'An' then—payday,' Kane growled with relish. 'Forty-five hunnerd bucks.'

'Plus a thousand-dollar bonus,' O'Brien reminded him with a smile. 'To be split equally between us. Remember?'

They both looked at Bruce-Morgan, who hesitated for just a moment before saying, 'Well... why not? I'd say you've earned it.'

Kane's teeth shone white through the gloom.

'Who's taking first watch?' O'Brien asked, changing the subject.

'Me, Ringgold an' Koch 'till midnight,' Kane replied. 'Then Coleman, Brand an' one o' th'Indians.'

O'Brien nodded and rose. 'Right, I'll leave

you to it, then.' He glanced up at the snow-spotted sky and jammed his fists deeper into the pockets of his sheepskin. 'You sure didn't kid me about the bad weather they have up here, Morgan. I didn't even see winters this bad when I was a kid back home in Colorado.'

The Scotsman chuckled. 'Well, maybe now you can understand why our supplies are worth so much more here than anywhere else,' he replied.

'I think I can at that.'

'Goodnight, O'Brien.'

' 'Night.'

Exhaling pale clouds of vapour into the darkness, the freelance fighting man traipsed over to the cowboys and gave tham a hand setting up their makeshift shelter, accepting their subsequent invitation to share the temporary accommodation gratefully.

Sometime around two o'clock the dogs began to bark and yap excitedly, waking O'Brien from a deep, cold-induced slumber.

For a time he lay in his soogans beneath the breeze-blown tarpaulin, listening to the night sounds; the odd cow-bellow and horse-nicker; the keening of the wind; Hermanas snoring; the gentle susurration of snow accumulating on the canvas above them.

166

Finally he rolled out of his blankets and grabbed his Winchester, then stepped over the sleeping men and knelt by the tent-entrance.

The campfire had burned down to embers, and fast-falling snow made visibility even worse. He squinted, straining to see across to the other side of the camp, then heard one of the Tlingits shout something in Chinook that quietened the dogs down.

O'Brien crouched there a moment longer, listening to the distant howling of wolves somewhere off in the timber. Then, when he was certain that everything was as it should be, he put the disturbance from his mind and went back to bed.

He rose again while dawn was still fifteen minutes away, dry-washed his eyes, combed his face and grabbed his hat. Stepping outside, he saw that the snow had let up for a while, although the low, grey-bellied clouds above promised more before noon. What little light there was shimmered and bounced off the fresh fall, giving the sheltered bowl an unreal, fairy-tale appearance.

Bruce-Morgan was hunkered over by the fire. He glanced up when he heard the small, satisfied sound O'Brien made stretching his spine. 'Morning,' he said. 'Coffee?'

167

'Uh-huh.' O'Brien came nearer and accepted a cup. Around them the rest of the crew stirred sluggishly beneath their blankets, doubtless trying to find the energy to get up and start a new, limit-pushing day. 'What's up? Couldn't sleep?'

Bruce-Morgan shook his head and smiled ruefully. 'Every time I closed my eyes I saw poor Ed,' he confessed.

'That's tough,' O'Brien remarked sympathetically. 'But you can't mourn the dead forever, Morgan. Oh, don't get me wrong. There's not a day gone by that I haven't remembered the look on Ed's face when he slipped out of this life and into the next. But there wasn't anything you or me or anybody else could have done to change that boy's fate.'

The Scotsman sighed. 'I guess you're right.'

'I am, believe me.'

'I'll be sending the money Ed would've earned on to his folks,' Bruce-Morgan said. 'That and a little something extra, by way of compensation. Tom Koch gave me their address.'

O'Brien nodded his approval. 'It might help,' he agreed. 'This—'

He was interrupted by a sudden yell from somewhere in among the trees. *'Quick!'*

'What the devil—?' Bruce-Morgan began, startled.

O'Brien dropped his mug into the snow and hurried across the camp towards the timber, hauling his Colt Lightning from leather just as the dogs started howling afresh. Somewhere up ahead the voice called out again. Its tone was panicky and urgent. O'Brien recognised it as belonging to Sam Coleman and ran faster.

Almost before he knew it Coleman appeared in front of him, and skidding to a halt, he looked into the man's deep-set blue eyes, seeing something wild and fearful there.

'What is it?' he snapped.

Coleman wheeled around, as if he'd heard a sound from someplace deeper in the woods. He held his Henry repeater business-end first, but somehow fought the urge to start blasting at shadows. 'Noatak!' he said just as O'Brien heard Bruce-Morgan, Kane and a few others dash up behind him.

Noatak was one of the Indian packers; the one who'd been assigned the midnight-to-six watch along with Coleman and Brand. 'What about him?' O'Brien demanded in a hiss.

Coleman turned back to him. 'He's dead!' he replied. 'Been *murdered.*'

There was a collective gasp behind O'Brien, but he paid it no attention. 'Where?' he asked tightly, eyes scouring their gloomy surroundings. 'Show me. And Ches—while I'm gone, take a couple of men and make sure whoever did the deed's not still around.'

'Yo!'

Kane rattled off a few names and the group split into two smaller parties, one to secure the area, the other to view the crime.

O'Brien, with Bruce-Morgan, Hermanas, Ringgold and about three of the Tlingits in tow, asked Coleman what had happened. As the grey-bearded wagon-driver led them along the northwest perimeter of the camp he said, 'I was standin' watch, just waitin' for the sun to come up, when I figured I'd take me a little wander, you know, jus' to stretch m'legs.'

'And that's when you found him?'

Coleman dipped his head. 'Damn' nigh tripped right over 'im,' he confirmed. ' 'Bout a second after that I started yellin', then came a-runnin'.'

Suddenly he pulled up sharp and pointed off into the trees on their left. O'Brien followed his gaze and saw the Indian curled into a ball about twelve or fifteen feet away.

He approached the body cautiously, but only one set of tracks had gouged twin furrows out of the foot-deep snow around Noatak; Coleman's. Any sign the Indian's killer might have left behind him last night had long since been erased by the most recent snowfall.

Feeling the eyes of his companions on him, O'Brien reached down and turned the Tlingit over. The poor fellow had been dead some time, and his coppery skin held a bluish tinge. His throat had been cut, and the blood around the wound had dried to a crusty black skin, dusted with ice.

O'Brien swore under his breath and turned to face the others, reporting the facts as he saw them. Then he asked Coleman, 'When did you last see him alive?'

'I dunno. 'Bout an hour after we came on watch, mebbe.'

O'Brien considered that. 'You didn't see him after, say, two o'clock, then?'

'Nope.'

'Why two o'clock?' asked Ringgold.

'Because it was around that time that the dogs went wild. Remember all that yapping? Maybe that's when the killer struck.'

'*Damn,*' muttered Hermanas.

'But who could have done it?' Bruce-Morgan asked, shaking his head in disbelief. 'I mean, *why?*'

O'Brien shrugged. 'Lord knows. But I sure aim to find...' He broke off suddenly, running his faded blue eyes across the row of faces watching him. 'Where's Ginny?' he asked softly.

A look of horror washed across the Scotsman's face as the implication behind O'Brien's question struck home. 'Oh my God,' he husked, turning back to camp. *'Ginny!'*

As one the small party stumbled back the way they'd come, kicking up small puffs of fallen snow as they waded quickly across the camp towards the silent Sibley tent.

'Ginny!'

There came no response.

They slurred to a halt in a ragged half-circle around the canvas shelter, all but Bruce-Morgan, who dropped to his knees and fumbled with the ties at the tent's entrance.

Panic made his fingers uncooperative. Mumbling incoherently he finally tore back one of the flaps and stuck his head and shoulder inside.

He stiffened, gasped and moaned.

Standing behind him, O'Brien's imagination conjured up a picture too awful to contemplate, and he pushed through the others rougher than he meant to, to kneel beside the Scotsman.

Forcing himself to speak, he said, 'What is it?'

Bruce-Morgan backed out of the Sibley tent and faced him, pale, haunted, in shock.

'Ginny,' he replied. 'She's not there, O'Brien! She's *disappeared!*'

172

O'Brien brushed him aside and took a look for himself. Now that the sun was rising, the tent was lit by a sickly green hue. One quick scan confirmed what the Scotsman had said. Apart from a rumpled mess of blankets, a vanity box and the faintest aroma of Ginny's perfume lingering on the bitter air, the tent *was* empty.

Then what in hell had become of the girl?

He was just about to withdraw back into the growing daylight when two things caught his eye—clues which, in his blue funk, Bruce-Morgan had overlooked.

One was a ragged slit in the tent's back wall, most likely made with the very same knife which had slit Noatak's throat.

The other was a note, folded into a two-inch square and all but lost in the tangled blankets.

As O'Brien reached down and plucked it up, his guts did a slow roll. Willing his heart to slow its hammering, he unfolded the scrap of paper and read the message printed neatly upon it.

It said:

BRUCE-MORGAN—
YOUR SISTER IS SAFE. TO GET HER BACK ALL YOU HAVE TO DO IS HAND YOUR STOCK OVER TO ME. RILEY WILL COLLECT AT NOON.

The note was signed with one initial.

G.

For *Goodlight*.

'Sonofabitch!' growled Coleman. He spoke for all the men, red *and* white, after Bruce-Morgan finished reading the note aloud for their information.

'It's clear enough how they did it,' Kane said, folding his arms across his narrow, bandolier-draped chest. 'One or more of Goodlight's hired guns snuck in 'round two o'clock this mornin', kilt the feller that wuz gardin' the stretch o' land closest to Miz Ginny's tent, then slit an entry-hole in the tent itself an' made off with her.'

'An' all the time, them dogs was tryin' to tell us,' Jack Brand added, realising just how close he himself had come to being killed.

'Question now,' Kane said, turning to the shattered Scotsman, 'is what're we gonna *do* 'bout it?'

Bruce-Morgan made a brave attempt to shake off his distress, but it was obvious that this new turn of events had knocked him sideways. 'Do? Why, there's no question, Ches. We're going to give Goodlight whatever it takes to get Ginny back!'

'You mean give *in* to 'em?' asked Coleman.

'Jus' like that?'

'Do you think we've got a choice?' the Scotsman snapped in reply, wringing his hands in agitation. 'If anything happens to my sister...' His eyes moved from one face to another, his vision slowly blurring with anxious tears. 'Gentlemen... she's all I have in the world.'

He bowed his head, screwing the note into a ball and letting it drop to the snow between his feet.

'Don't fret, *senor*,' said Felipe Hermanas, breaking the embarrassing silence. He glanced to left and right, at the men flanking him. 'It'll work out. You'll see. We'll do like you say. Give Goodlight what he wants. And once we've got your sister back, we'll—'

'We'll do nothing,' O'Brien cut in, speaking for the first time. As all heads swung his way he said grimly, 'Because we won't *get* Ginny back. Leastways not straightaway.'

'You mean... you mean Goodlight will keep her? As a... a hostage?' Bruce-Morgan said in despair.

'Something like that. Call it "insurance", if you like. To make sure we don't try anything sudden to get the supplies back again.'

'Then what *can* we do?' the Scotsman implored. 'I *have* to give him what he wants. I don't dare risk doing anything else.'

175

O'Brien met his bloodshot eyes and held them with his own intense stare. 'Oh, you'll do what he wants, all right,' he agreed in a low, tight voice. 'And you'll do whatever he tells you, too.'

'But...?' prodded Kane, stepping closer.

O'Brien eyed him sidelong. 'But,' he replied, 'I *won't*.'

The negro frowned. 'Maybe you'd better explain that,' he said.

O'Brien did.

'*No!*' Bruce-Morgan breathed at the end of it. 'No, I won't allow it, O'Brien! It's too risky—and I won't jeopardise Ginny's life! I—'

'Shaddup,' Kane snapped, surprising the Scotsman into silence. 'Don't you understan' sense when you hear it? You let Harvey Goodlight get away with this now an' he'll be pullin' your string from now till Judgement Day. At least the way O'Brien tells it we got a *chance* of gettin' even with the sumbitch—gettin' Miss Ginny'n them supplies back in one piece, too.'

Bruce-Morgan bowed his head. 'I just...' He shrugged helplessly.

'Trust me, Morgan,' O'Brien urged softly. 'I haven't let you down yet.'

'But are you sure it'll work?' the Scotsman asked in a cracked, desperate tone.

O'Brien shook his head. 'Not sure, no,' he replied candidly. 'But one thing I *will* guarantee you—that I'll be giving it everything I've got.'

Goodlight's men turned up just a couple of minutes before noon.

Riley was in the lead, astride a muscular buckskin, and eight hardcases were fanned out behind him, stirrup to stirrup, their long-guns resting within easy reach across their saddlehorns.

Bruce-Morgan, Kane and the others stood in silence, watching them come closer through a screen of slowly-falling snow, eyes smarting, breath misting. They heard the low, ominous jingle and creak of harness and leather, and the soft but relentless *shush-shush* of horse-hoof through snow. They looked into the flat, life-is-cheap eyes of Goodlight's hired guns, and not one of them, save maybe Kane, felt entirely fearless in their presence.

They came deeper into the sheltered bowl.

Riley's buffalo-hide coat made him look twice his size. His plainsman's hat, glistening with fallen snow, threw shadow over his ugly face. As he and his men rode closer, the haggard Scotsman saw his wide, cocksure grin clearly, heard the sound he made humming, and bunched his fists at his sides.

'Easy does it,' warned Kane, standing next to him.

Riley brought his buckskin to a halt about twenty feet away. Behind him his men reined in, too. The runty little gunman leaned forward to rest his forearms on his saddle-horn, and ran his coal-black eyes over the line of men in front of him: the Scotsman, the negro, the wagon-drivers, the cowboys, the Tlingits.

He stopped humming and frowned.

'Where's O'Brien?' he demanded.

Bruce-Morgan almost didn't hear him over the pounding of blood in his ears. He opened his mouth to reply but couldn't speak. To cover for him Kane said, 'Where's Miss *Ginny?*'

Riley's eyes never left Bruce-Morgan's face. 'I ast you a question,' he muttered in a low, impatient voice.

'He's dead,' the Scotsman said at last. Clearing his throat, he went on, 'And as Chester just said—where is my sister?'

But Riley wasn't listening. *'Dead?'* he repeated sceptically. He nudged his horse nearer, the look on his face a compound of emotions: surprise, caution, disappointment at having been cheated out of his own personal revenge.

Bruce-Morgan drew in one breath. Another.

178

For one hideous moment he didn't think he was going to be able to carry the plan through. Then he pictured Ginny in his mind. The distress he himself was experiencing now was as nothing compared to that of his sister. If she could cope with it—and he was sure that she *could*—then so could he.

'Yes, *dead*,' he replied, allowing his impatience to combat his anxiety. 'It happened about a week and a half ago. His horse slipped in a snowdrift and the pair of them went down in a tangle. O'Brien was... was crushed.'

Somehow he forced himself to meet Riley's furious stare. Then Goodlight's foreman eyed each of the others in turn. Only Ringgold shuffled his feet. 'You're lyin',' he growled at last.

'We buried him,' Bruce-Morgan replied sharply, 'in a stand of timber about thirty miles north of Yacutat.'

He watched Riley's face closely now, searching for a reaction, and found one in the sudden twitch of Riley's left cheek and the flaring of his nostrils. Riley had seen the grave beneath the trees all those miles behind them, he felt certain. And unless he'd disinterred the body, he wasn't to know that it actually marked the final resting-place of Ed Harper.

But he still wasn't entirely convinced. Turning his face into profile he said over his shoulder, 'Wayne, Barton, Marshall, Grover; search this place. If this is some trick, an' O'Brien's lurkin' around here somewhere, I want him found.'

'I'd hardly be likely to do anything so foolish while you're holding my sister captive!' Bruce-Morgan flared.

Riley eyed him sidelong. 'We'll search *anyway*,' he decided.

The four hardcases he'd named dismounted and set about the task, watched by the Scotsman's silent crew. As the snow gradually began to let up and the milky sky cleared a little, they checked the tent, the makeshift shelter, the sleds, the trees, the rocks; even in among the horses, the dogs and the cattle.

'He ain't here,' a man with an old knife-scar running down his left cheek finally announced.

'The only body *I* found,' said another equally-unlovely specimen, 'was that Injun Grover done for when we snatched the girl las' night.'

Riley glanced around them, not replying straightaway. Melting snow slid down his coat and trickled across his horse's grey-yellow flanks. 'If this *is* some kind of a trick...' he began. Then he reached a decision in his mind, no doubt prodded along by a desire to get, moving and out of this weather. Dismounting, he waded across to Bruce-Morgan, dragging a scrap of paper from his right-side pocket. 'This here's a bill o'sale,' he explained. 'Once you've signed it you an' your men can head back to Yacutat. The Injuns'll stay with us.'

'What about my sister?' Bruce-Morgan husked.

'She'll stay with us, too,' Riley replied. 'Just to make sure you do like I say.' His grin was insolent. 'Oh, don't worry; she'll be in good hands—I'll see to that personally.'

'Why you—'

'You'll get her back once we've sold the stock an' started back to Seattle,' Riley continued. 'An' don't try anythin' dumb, Morgan, 'cause we'll have a man or two doggin' you all the time, just to make sure you don't try doublin' back.'

'If you harm Ginny—'

Riley lashed out with blinding speed, the knuckles of his gloved right hand crashing into the Scotsman's square jaw. Bruce-Morgan made a small sound of surprise and went down onto his knees. When he squinted up at his attacker, a thick worm of blood spilled sluggishly down his chin and tears shone in his eyes.

'I got no time fer fools as waste their breath makin' idle threats,' he growled brusquely. 'Just sign the bill o'sale an' get the hell outta here.'

He tossed the document down to Bruce-Morgan and the Scotsman picked it up with a trembling hand. According to the crude but nonetheless legal certificate Harvey Goodlight had drawn up, Bruce-Morgan had sold his entire stock two weeks earlier, for a total price of five thousand dollars, which had already been paid in full. There was a space for Bruce-Morgan's signature, which one of Goodlight's cronies—the man Benteen—had already witnessed.

Riley threw him a stub of pencil. 'Sign it,' he barked.

Bruce-Morgan fumbled the pencil up from out of the snow and flattened the bill of sale against one bent knee. Before he did as he had been told, however, he glanced up at Kane, then across to Coleman, Ringgold and the others.

'I'm sorry,' he mumbled.

Then he endorsed the document.

It took a time to get everything prepared, but within the half-hour Bruce-Morgan and his six companions were mounted up and heading back south with heads down and defeated. Riley watched them go, humming, then turned his beady eyes on the seven sullen-looking Tlingits who had, at his bidding, stayed behind.

'Any o'you fellers speak English?' he demanded.

A raven-haired fellow named Coho said that he did.

'Well, pass this along to your buddies,' Riley replied. 'From now on, you're workin' fer *me*. Keep your noses clean an' you'll have no trouble. Try makin' life hard an' I'll kill every mother's son of you, I swear it. Now—get them dogs into their traces. We got a man to meet 'bout three, four miles north o'here, an' I don't want to keep him waitin'!'

Coho turned to his copper-faced brothers and translated. Slowly, and with barely-controlled anger, the Tlingits began to ready their laden sleds for travel.

Ignoring the murderous looks they directed his way, Riley barked, 'Barton!'

The man who came over to him was tall and loose-limbed, with a broad, pugilist's face and a thick black moustache. Like his companions he wore a heavy greatcoat, and the Montana peak atop his head was tied down with a wool scarf. 'Yeah?' A cloud of vapour poured from his mouth.

'Shadow that Scotsman,' Riley told him. 'Make sure he does what he's been told. If it looks like he's gonna come after us, hole up someplace high and use that rifle o'yourn to pick off a couple of his partners, just to dissuade 'im. Got it?'

Barton nodded. 'Got it.'

Riley watched him stump back across to his horse, unsheath his Winchester and check its action. It was too bad about O'Brien, he thought, recalling the lonely grave he and the others had found several days earlier. He'd been looking forward to making that sonofa-bitch pay. Still, he'd got what was coming to him in the end, he guessed. And that was all that mattered.

As he headed back to his own horse he resumed humming.

NINE

Driving the cattle ahead of them, Riley's men followed the sleds north through the rocks, leaving the sheltered bowl silent and empty.

About five minutes passed. Nothing moved to disturb the stillness. Then, slowly, the body of the dead Indian, Noatak, began to... *shift.*

Before long the sprawled corpse rolled onto its side as the ground beneath it began to rearrange itself. As the subterranean movements grew more pronounced, so great clods of snow began to crack apart and slide aside, revealing an olive-green tarpaulin beneath.

O'Brien pushed the canvas cover aside and crawled out from his hiding-place. Then he straightened to his full height. He was more cramped than cold, and now he flexed his fingers, kicked his legs, stretched his arms and drew deeply on the chill, fresh air.

He glanced around the camp. After the smooth white snowfields he'd grown used to, the churned-up slush that met his gaze now seemed ugly. But in a way it figured. Men like Goodlight and Riley spoiled whatever they came into contact with.

And that was why they had to be stopped.

Ploughing through the snow with arms outstretched for balance, he reached the centre of the basin and bent to inspect the tracks Riley's men had left behind them. Although sound hadn't carried all that well to his temporary hideout, he'd heard enough, when Riley had raised his voice to talk to the Tlingits, to know that Goodlight—and presumably, Ginny—had swung out ahead of them and would be found three or four miles further north. The clearly-defined tracks to be read in the snow told him that Riley had dispatched one of his gunhawks to follow Bruce-Morgan.

O'Brien decided that he would be taken out of the picture first.

He glanced up at the sky. Here and there a little blue showed through the grey. Unless he was mistaken, it looked as if the clearer weather might hold for a while. Good.

He splashed back the way he'd come, going deeper into the cool, quiet shadows of the timber. The snow, blocked by the interlacing branches above, hadn't penetrated this stretch of ground, so his progress was both fast and unhindered.

He covered about half a mile or just under before he came to the animals he had tethered

186

to a fallen tree earlier on. His own quarter-horse bobbed its head and nickered a greeting when he came into sight. Chester Kane's flop-eared mule, still toting the gear that constituted the black man's old Army keepsake, paid him no attention whatsoever.

Mounting up and wrapping the mule's rein around his free left hand, O'Brien started his horse southeast. Figuring distances in his mind, he guessed that Bruce-Morgan's band would be about two miles away by now; Riley's man—if he had any sense—no more than a quarter-mile behind them.

O'Brien wanted to catch up with that man. *Bad.*

His years as a professional soldier of fortune had prepared him for this moment. He knew exactly what he had to do, and exactly how to do it, too. His speed was moderate but constant. His eyes rarely focused for long on any one place. Soon he left the timber behind him and cut sign. For long, cold minutes he studied the track-patterned snow. The Scotsman had passed this way some time before. Riley's man, too, judging by the tracks off to one side of the trail.

That meant they were all up ahead someplace.

187

Clucking his horse back into motion, O'Brien followed the tracks, riding with more caution now. The thin black hands of the gold Hunter watch in his pants'-pocket moved slowly from 2:20 to 3:05. Then O'Brien reined in, narrowing his scratchy eyes.

Because Riley's man, Barton, was about three hundred yards ahead.

Quickly swinging his horse off the trail and in among some snow-topped boulders, O'Brien cooled his saddle, ground-hitched both animals, fumbled his field glasses from his saddlebags and began to scramble up a white slope in order to spy on the other man. When he found the right spot, he bellied-down in the snow, put the binoculars to his eyes and slowly pulled Barton into focus.

Up ahead the trail tapered down to a width of no more than fifteen feet. To either side rose gentle, snow-patched hills littered with bushes, Siberian asters, prickly white roses and rocks, from small grey pebbles to huge, coffee-coloured boulders.

Beyond the narrow pass rose the tall mountains in which Bruce-Morgan's band had found the frozen cheekako. The peaks fairly soared towards the slowly-darkening sky.

Barton had dismounted and was holding his calico mare by its rein. As near as O'Brien

188

could judge, he appeared to be watching something up ahead; almost likely the Scotsman's party, who had probably called a halt to make camp before full dark descended.

O'Brien felt the coldness of the snow beneath him bouncing up to tighten his already windburnt face. But he lay where he was a moment longer, deciding what to do next. Barton had to be taken out fast, and quietly. O'Brien didn't want any gunshots putting Riley on his guard. That meant the fighting would be hand-to-hand, then.

Shoving himself up off the snow ridge, he began to crouch-walk along the elevated slope, keeping to the rocks and stunted trees until he reached a place where he could look down on the brawny hardcase, and track his field glasses further south to locate Bruce-Morgan and Co., who were indeed fixing camp in a stand of timber beside a frozen stream about half a mile away.

Returning his magnified lenses to Barton, he found the man preparing to remount. Chances were that the gunman wanted to get in closer before making his own night-camp.

Quickly O'Brien scanned the slope below him and to his right. If he could just make it down to the rocky overhang about ninety or a hundred yards to the south and east—

Rather than waste time thinking about it, O'Brien left the field glasses where they were and began to angle towards his new destination, relying on the thick cover and lowering light to hide him from his quarry.

Somehow he managed to keep from slipping during his skittering, headlong descent of the brush-bearded slope. Down below and about a hundred and fifty feet to his left, Barton climbed back into the saddle and heeled his horse into a high-stepping trot.

Then O'Brien felt the ground level out beneath him and went down as quietly as he could, feeling the cold, seamed rock even through his gloves. The overhang shelved partway across the trail, which wound past about ten or twelve feet below.

Twisting his head to the left, he watched Barton urging his calico nearer. *This is it*, he thought, slowly bringing his legs up beneath him.

The horse carried its master closer, harness jingling softly.

When Barton was abreast of the formation, O'Brien launched himself into mid-air. Barton, seeing something from the corner of his eye and thinking it to be a wolf or a grizzly, hipped around and loosed a startled oath.

Before he could say much more than *'Wha—?'*

however, O'Brien grabbed him around the neck, and Barton's boots parted company with his stirrups as both men crashed to the ground and the calico pranced aside, rearing nervously.

For a moment the two men rolled over in a wild tangle of arms and legs. Then Barton broke the strangle-hold and lurched to his feet, aiming a kick at O'Brien's face.

O'Brien caught the boot, twisted it and Barton went over again. Before he could rise, O'Brien fairly leapt on him and rammed his face into the snow.

As the snow filled his mouth and nostrils, Barton struggled beneath him. His legs kicked. His fists beat at the ground. He tried to twist around but O'Brien, teeth clenched, pushed him even deeper into the snow.

After what seemed like an age, the hardcase began to struggle less and less as he slowly suffocated in the freezing ice crystals. Five minutes later a shudder ran the length of his body and O'Brien knew that he was dead.

Pushing himself away from the corpse, he drew in a deep breath. The type of death he'd inflicted upon Barton had left him trembling. Bending, he retrieved his hat, which had fallen off during the brief fray, and went across to the still-spooked horse.

'Go on, get out of here!' he yelled, slapping

the critter on the rump.

The horse took off along the trail, hooves kicking up a spray of snow as it disappeared into the gloom. With any luck it would reach Bruce-Morgan's camp within the half-hour, and the Scotsman would realise that its owner was no longer in any position to follow them.

Climbing back up the slope to retrieve his field glasses, the blue-eyed fighting man retraced his steps still further until he came to his horse and the mule. Now that he'd taken care of Barton, it was time to see what he could do for Ginny.

Night had already fallen by the time he angled the horse back out onto the trail, but the clouds had cleared sufficiently to allow the light of a bloated hunter's moon to shimmer and reflect off the settled snow all around him. Furthermore, as O'Brien trotted the horse north, back to the sheltered bowl and beyond, the *aurora borealis* added a myriad of colours to the soft, spectral glow, taking his mind off the bloodletting that still lay ahead.

Now that he was no longer burdened by ten sleds and a hundred-plus beeves, he moved quickly over the inhospitable terrain. With Polaris, the North Star, to guide him, he soon arrived back at the basin, and once there, paused long enough to spell the horses, start a small fire and boil up some coffee and beans.

It had been a long day, he thought, as he rubbed at his eyes. Cold, too; so cold, in fact, that if he were to spit, O'Brien reckoned that his saliva would freeze solid before it hit the ground. To keep warm he saw to the comfort of the animals, then hunkered beside the welcome flames and allowed himself a light but refreshing doze.

He was about half-way through a plate of beans when his ears picked out the sound of a man trying to approach him stealthily from the south. Transferring his plate to his left hand and drawing his Colt with the right, he said, 'You oughta know better than to creep up on a man like that, Kane.'

A grim chuckle floated out of the darkness directly ahead. A moment later Chester Kane followed it, leading his *grulla* by the rein and holding his Winchester at his side.

'You took your time, didn't you?' O'Brien remarked, putting the gun away and ladling beans onto a second plate.

Kane only shrugged and loosened his horse's cinch-strap. 'Left just as soon's that hoss you sent down the trail come a-bustin' into our camp,' he replied, taking the food with a nod of thanks.

'Well, eat up quick; we'll move out again in

fifteen minutes.' O'Brien finished chewing and set his own plate aside. 'The others'll meet us here sometime tomorrow, right?' he asked absently as he rose to scan the surrounding shadows.

'Jus' like you told 'em,' Kane responded. 'They'll stay where they is tonight, set out come sun-up, an' biv'uac heah 'til we bring Miss Ginny back to 'em.' He cleaned his plate, then sharpened his dark gaze on O'Brien's back. 'Talking' o' which,' he said quietly. 'You got any notion jus' how we're gonna do that small thing yet?'

O'Brien shook his head. 'Nope,' he replied without taking his eyes off the churned-up snow to the north, which marked the passage of the Herefords. 'But I'll think of something when the time comes.'

Kane snorted. 'Hell, boy,' he muttered. 'You'd *better*.'

A quarter-hour later they were back in the saddle and leading the mule along the ugly road of mulched snow in search of their prey.

O'Brien was confident that Goodlight wouldn't have gone far. The slow-moving cattle, the early darkness and the uncooperative Tlingets would've made certain of that. So catching up with their opponents would be no

194

problem; managing to get Ginny out of their clutches unharmed... that was something *else*.

The trail was so prominent now that even a blind man could have followed it without working up a sweat. It wound in wide, lazy half-moons across the rumpled, tree-spiked tundra for one mile, three, five, seven.

It was sometime around midnight when the bawling of the cattle told them that they'd finally reached their destination, and quickly reining in, they ground-hobbled their animals and covered what remained of the slushy trail on foot.

The now-frozen tracks led them up a gentle, timbered slope. They went belly-down before reaching the top, and shucked their headgear prior to chancing a look over the rim.

Straight ahead, dominating the vista and standing dark against the clear, star-packed night sky, lay the foothills of the smallest range of mountains O'Brien had so far seen in Alaska. Although it was difficult to judge distances in such poor light, he guessed they must lay between three and five miles away. Wisely, Goodlight had called a halt in the valley leading up to the peaks rather than risk pushing on in darkness.

Gently, so's not to cause any more noise than he had to, O'Brien reached into his sheepskin

195

jacket and brought out his field glasses. The metal eye-rims felt cold as he held them close to his skin.

The cattle, he saw, had been driven down the far slope in a fairly straight line, and once reaching the bottom, had been forced to cut a path through thick timber and rocks. The trail they'd left behind them was maybe thirty feet wide, certainly no more. To either side of it rose more gentle hills, barbed with stunted pines and spruce, goose-bumped with rocks.

Goodlight's camp lay about a hundred yards northwest, just off the main trace. It was about the only cleared area large enough to rest the men and beasts comfortably. Training his lenses on that tract, O'Brien saw the shadowy, moon-silvered backs of milling cattle about a hundred and twenty feet north of the small fire crackling at the centre of camp. Moving the binoculars slowly in a northwest-to-south arc, he picked out the huddled malemutes... the sleeping Tlingits... the canvas-covered sleds ...a small pup-tent that might have housed Ginny or Goodlight or God forbid, both...

Tracking his vision back to the camp-fire, he began to count the men sleeping nearby. He paused at five.

Five.

Supposing he allowed for another couple

keeping guard, two more riding nighthawk on the herd...

Nine men minimum, then.

He passed the field glasses to Kane. 'Here, see what you make of it.'

A moment later Kane pursed his lips but refrained from whistling. 'This is gonna be tricky,' he decided.

'No it isn't,' O'Brien replied firmly. 'It's gonna be easy—as simple as going in, grabbing Ginny and hauling her right out of there.'

'Huh? Are you crazy—?'

O'Brien turned to face him. Through the gloom all he could detect were Kane's eyes. 'It's *got* to be simple,' he argued in a harsh whisper. 'We haven't got the time for anything fancier.'

Kane let out a stream of cloudy breath. 'What 'bout them Injuns?' he asked. 'Happen you *do* get Miss Ginny outta theah, Goodlight's still got them Tlingits to bargain with.'

'Has he? An Indian's just an Indian to a man like Goodlight. He'd never even *dream* Bruce-Morgan could give a damn about 'em.'

'Well...' Kane made a gesture of frustration with the hand holding the binoculars. 'What if it comes to shootin'?' he demanded. 'Happen them beeves down theah spook, they'll scatter all over this valley.'

197

'They won't run far in this country,' O'Brien predicted. 'Hell, it's all they can do to walk.'

'But, dammit, O'Brien—'

'Get your little Army keepsake set up on this ridge, Ches,' O'Brien muttered, paying the other man no attention. 'Just in case.'

The black man's teeth appeared briefly in a grin. 'Sure,' he replied laconically. 'Just in case you get yo' crazy white ass blowed off.' He peered up at the sky. 'When you figure on sashayin' down theah, anyway?'

O'Brien started to edge away from the rim. 'First light,' he replied grimly.

O'Brien set out about an hour before dawn, snaking over the ridge, down the slope and into the trees leading to the campsite, figuring to have two big advantages over Goodlight and Riley.

For one thing, while they might expect Ginny to make an attempt at escape, it was unlikely that they would plan on someone coming in to fetch her. For another; as far as they were concerned, O'Brien was dead.

Still, if things didn't go according to plan, his return from the grave might prove to be only temporary. He kept that thought in mind as he snuck closer.

As Kane had rightly said, his plan was crazy.

But what other options were there? Goodlight wasn't going to release the girl until he was well on his way back to Seattle, and even then there was no guarantee that he would set her free unscathed. Oh, he himself might draw the line at rape, sure—but would Riley, or his fellow cut-throats?

O'Brien made it deeper into the timber, moving slowly, taking care to hug cover and keep as silent as possible.

By the time he made it to the far edge of the woods, he was almost directly behind the pup-tent, which stood about thirty feet away. Crouching, he listened to the restless shifting of the cattle, the odd cough, fart, muttering and horse-nicker. A little further over, some of the malemutes, perhaps catching his scent on the bitter breeze, started howling.

'*Shaddup!*' called a man patrolling the perimeter about sixty feet away. '...damn' hounds...'

Cautiously O'Brien got his feet under him and eased his jack-knife from one pocket. But as luck would have it, the hardcase was ambling away from him.

Peering into the darkness in the opposite direction, he satisfied himself that he was, for the time being at least, alone.

Without stopping to think about it—and consequently pausing to await a better chance that might never come—he slithered across the snowy ground that separated the trees from the tent and came up sharp beside the canvas. Once there he took another look around. Still all quiet.

Straining his ears, he tried to catch any tell-tale sounds that might emanate from within the tent, but all was silent. Was Ginny in there? If so, was she *alone?* And if she *was* alone, would she herself unwittingly raise the alarm when he attempted to rescue her? Damn. There were so many questions, and only one way to answer them.

As the sun began to fight its way over the treetops to the east and turn the black sky grey, he clenched his teeth, stabbed his knife through the canvas tent-back and drew it down in one sharp motion, creating a ragged slit.

Reaching in fast, he clamped one hand over the face of the figure now stirring beneath the blankets. The figure struggled, made a small, frightened noise, opened its eyes—

—and O'Brien saw himself reflected in Ginny's hazel orbs.

It took her another frantic, struggling moment to recognise him. When at last she did, all movement within her ceased.

'Come on,' he whispered urgently. 'We're

getting out of here!'

'O'Brien! What—I mean, how—'

'Later!'

'I can't—I—I'm tied!'

Cursing softly, he squirmed deeper into the tent, pulled the blankets aside and quickly cut the ropes at her ankles. Then he rolled her over and sawed through the hemp holding her hands at the base of her spine.

'Come on now, quickly!'

He backed out of the tent and came up into a crouch. Putting the knife away, he drew his Colt. Not very far away he heard a small metallic scrape. He tensed, then relaxed a shade. Judging from the rich smell of Arbuckle on the wind, one of the men sleeping around the fire had woken up and started coffee boiling in a pan.

He peered back down at the tent. 'Come *on*, dammit!'

Twenty seconds ticked into history before she crawled out of the tent. She was fully-dressed, but dangerously pale through the semi-darkness, her hair a mess, her mouth a down-turned horseshoe reflecting her fear and apprehension.

'Into the trees,' he hissed.

'Is—?'

'Just *do* it!'

201

Before she could move, however, he clamped his left hand around one of her arms and held her where she was. Another of Goodlight's men had risen and was stamping off through the snow to urinate in the rocks to the west. Yawning and obviously still befuddled by sleep, the man fumbled at his pants'-buttons.

Controlling his breathing, O'Brien gently urged Ginny forward. 'Now,' he whispered.

There was no help for the small, crunching sound they made ploughing back across the snow to the timber. O'Brien just hoped the hardcases were still too sluggish to hear them.

Too bad that they weren't.

'Hey—you!'

O'Brien snapped his head around and cursed. It was the man patrolling the perimeter seventy feet away who'd raised the alarm. Maybe he'd heard them. Maybe he'd turned and seen them. Either way, O'Brien's immediate reaction was to push Ginny on ahead and yell, *'Run!'*

'But—'

'That way!' he bellowed, pointing. 'You'll find Kane about a hundred yards south!'

She froze for just a second as he twisted around to face the guard who was now approaching them at a run. Even as the fellow brought his rifle up, O'Brien snap-aimed the

202

Colt and shot him twice in the chest. As he flew over backwards, she finally turned and did as he'd told her, high-stepping through the snow to reach the cover of the trees.

By now the early-morning air was filled with noise; men yelling, dogs barking, cattle bawling and guns blasting. One of Goodlight's men, just in the act of drawing his Remington .44, suddenly felt a hand clamp over his mouth, haul back and snap his neck. Standing over him, one of the Tlingits, wearing a broad, fierce grin, snatched up the fallen handgun.

His triumph was short-lived, however. Almost as soon as he straightened up again, his coppery face burst apart in a crimson spray. Riley, lurching up from some blankets beside the fire, had spotted the potential rebellion about to begin and shot him as an example to the others.

As the Tlingit keeled over, Riley yelled, 'Tayler, Horn! Keep these bastards covered! Rest o'you men, follow me!'

Harvey Goodlight, kicking his own covers aside, watched the little man crash into the woods through which Ginny, and now her rescuer, had just disappeared.

There was a strange, scared look in Goodlight's shifty green eyes. He hadn't seen the man who'd pulled off the rescue. But he didn't have to. His lips narrowed down to a thin line and he snatched up a heavy buffalo-gun which had belonged to one of the dead men as he said the name once in his mind.

O'Brien.

'I knowed it! I jus' *knowed* it!'

Up until the gunfire began to pepper the silent morning air, Kane had just started to convince himself that maybe O'Brien *could* pull it off. After all, he'd done okay during the sea battle. He'd called it right with them two sour-doughs, Jones and Curry. And he'd certainly dealt with Barton in a permanent enough fashion.

So maybe he *could* get Miss Ginny out of Goodlight's camp before it came to more fighting.

Such optimistic thoughts were running through the black man's mind as he busied himself setting up the weapon he'd... *appropriated* from the Fort Denning arsenal before quitting New Mexico once and for all.

It was a beautiful machine, he decided, as he checked the action and found it in perfect working order. Just beautiful. He loaded the ammunition with swift, easy movements, then patted the top of the lightly-oiled killing-machine fondly.

And that was when the first of the gunshots cracked across the valley.

'Damn!'

Kane hurried down-slope to the hobbled horses, dragged his Winchester '73 from its scabbard and fought his way back up to the snowy rim again. The gunfire was becoming more regular now, all-but drowning the baying of the dogs and the low, mournful bellowing of the Herefords.

Jacking a shell into the long-gun, Kane narrowed his eyes and scanned the timberline. His first impulse was to go on down there and give O'Brien a hand. But as a soldier of many years' standing, he knew better than to desert his post.

Still...

He stiffened as a sudden flash of colour caught his eye. His dusky head snapped towards the northwest. Again! Someone was running hell-for-leather through them trees a couple hundred feet away.

Coming this way.

Well—if it wasn't Ginny, and it wasn't O'Brien...

Slowly he brought the Winchester stock up to his right cheek.

But then he relaxed his pressure on the trigger as Ginny came racing out of the trees and slipped in the icy, churned-up trail the cattle had left behind them the day before. She spilled onto all fours; Kane heard the shocked gasp she gave; then she shoved herself up and kept running.

'*Heah*, Miss Ginny! Up*heah!*'

He didn't think she heard him at first, so he waved with the Winchester to attract her attention. She was about a hundred and fifty feet away now; too far to tell for certain what was going through her mind. But then she looked up, saw him sky-lined clearly, broke stride for a moment, recovered herself and kept her long legs pumping.

Two heartbeats later O'Brien followed her out of the woods and onto the cattle-trail. The blue-eyed soldier of fortune turned once, emptied his Colt into the trees, then continued running towards the ridge.

'*Come on!*' Kane roared. '*Come on!*'

Ginny made it up the slope, her pale face streaked with dried tears and her hair a wild auburn tangle. Kane reached out, grabbed her and hauled her over the rim, behind him.

But O'Brien was still about a hundred feet away, and his pursuers had just burst out of the timber. Riley was in the lead; five other hardcases soon bunched themselves around him. Bringing the Winchester up to shoulder height, Kane fired one discouraging shot, another, another—

Riley and his cronies broke apart at this new attack. Kane gave a crazy whoop and levelled the long-gun for another fusillade. Before he could trigger it, however, one of the hardcases —Marshall—brought his own Spencer up, started firing back—and got lucky.

Kane gave a grunt and shrugged, dropping his rifle and tumbling backwards with blood coursing from a wound in his left hip. As he slid head first down the slope, Ginny screamed and threw herself towards him to arrest his fall.

Just as she got his head cradled in her lap, O'Brien made it over the rim, dimly aware of the triumphant shouts coming from the men behind him. 'Is he dead?' he barked, snatching up the other man's fallen rifle.

Before Ginny could reply, Kane opened his eyes. His dark skin looked ashen. 'Not yet,' he gritted.

O'Brien felt a brief surge of relief. Then he snapped his attention back to the six figures now storming the slope at a run, setting up a barrage of covering fire even though they were confident that O'Brien was out of ammunition and defenceless.

Tossing the rifle aside, he decided to give

207

them a surprise.

He turned his gaze onto Kane's Army keepsake—a Maxim heavy machine-gun.

The automatic weapon was mounted on a sturdy tripod. Its thick, dangerous-looking barrel protruded through a small oval shield which was designed to protect the user from return fire. The ammo was belt-fed; 333 gleaming Lebel cartridges shone one every three-quarters of an inch along a seven-yard belt that led up from a foot-long box beside the weapon in such a way that it would feed through the breech from left to right.

Throwing himself behind the gun, he grasped the handles, took aim and squeezed the trigger.

He was ready for the booming thunder of gunfire. That sound was an old companion. But nothing on earth could have prepared him for the machine-gun's awesome capabilities.

The Maxim leapt and jumped within his grasp as it fired ten shots every second. The belt chattered through the breech. Spent cartridge-cases flew through the cold air to his left. Flame belched from the muzzle as he sprayed the oncoming gunmen with a merciless hail of lead.

Riley got the first line of .75 calibre bullets. They stitched him across the chest and virtually tore him in half. But even before he dropped crimson to the snow, O'Brien turned the weapon onto the dead man's comrades.

Heat flooded up from the Maxim. The belt continued unwinding from the box to his right. On the slope ahead of him his hard-eyed enemies jerked and danced, screamed and spun, spat blood and fell writhing.

When he finally took his finger off the trigger, the machine-gun fell silent. He stood up, arms numb, and surveyed the scene of carnage below him.

Not one of the gunmen had survived the withering fire. They lay crumpled, bloodstained, twitching but already dead.

He sagged a little, and drew in a deep, exhausted breath. Killing always wearied him; not physically, but mentally.

But the killing wasn't finished yet.

Judging from the sounds of gunfire and screaming that now carried from the campsite, the Tlingets had somehow overcome what remained of their captors, and were exacting a bloody revenge. Good luck to them, he thought.

O'Brien glanced over his shoulder. Ginny had peeled back Kane's off-white duster and was examining the wound. The black man himself appeared to be asleep, his breathing shallow.

'Here,' O'Brien said, turning and hustling down the slope to join her. 'Let's get him turned around, make him more—'

A voice above them said, 'Don't move a muscle!'

O'Brien froze. With an empty gun in his holster and no other weapon within easy reach, he couldn't very well do much else. His eyes met Ginny's. Her face was slack with shock. Slowly he twisted his head in order to see Harvey Goodlight skylining himself clearly on the ridge twenty feet above and behind them, a Sharps Big Fifty in his hands and murder in his eyes.

'Stand up,' the Port Angeles entrepreneur commanded. 'Both of you!'

O'Brien ignored him. 'It's over, Goodlight. Can't you—'

'Stand up, I said!'

Together O'Brien and Ginny did as they were told, turning around cautiously in order to face their executioner head-on.

Goodlight stood with his legs spread apart for balance, the buffalo-gun braced against his right hip. His face was red, burned by the Arctic wind, and his expression was contorted. He wore a thick, ankle-length grey overcoat, *mukluks* and his familiar muley hat atop his macassared black hair.

210

'An interesting weapon,' he said, indicating the Maxim with a nod. 'As an ace in the hole, somewhat difficult to beat.'

O'Brien said, 'Throw down that gun, Goodlight. It's over.'

Goodlight nodded. 'You're right,' he agreed. 'It *is* over. For the two of *you*.'

'The girl doesn't have to be a part of it,' O'Brien told him quietly.

Goodlight's only response was to jerk the barrel of the Big Fifty to the right. 'Step across to that cleared area there. Lively, now! That's it.' His voice took on a hint of regret. 'You know, you could have become a rich man working for me, O'Brien,' he said. 'But now all you'll be is a dead one. Still, if it's any consolation, you *did* win the battle, even if you didn't win the war.'

He raised the buffalo gun. 'Bruce-Morgan can have his infernal supplies,' he said bitterly. 'Let him do with them as he will. Once he's got over the shock of finding your dead bodies, that is.'

He took up first pressure on the buffalo-gun's trigger. Fearing the worst, Ginny reached up to grasp O'Brien's left arm. One second later, a gunshot echoed across the empty, snow-buried land, and Ginny twitched and screamed.

But to their utter surprise, it was Goodlight

211

who collapsed, falling back over the ridge with a .476-inch slug from Chester Kane's Eley stuck in his throat.

The black man dropped his handgun and flopped back in the snow. In spite of the intense cold, sweat pebbled his forehead. 'Hot damn,' he muttered as O'Brien and Ginny splashed over to kneel beside him. 'Feel... weak as a kitten...'

O'Brien examined him closely. The wound in his side must hurt like a bitch, but he'd seen worse. 'All right, Ches,' he said. 'Just lay still. Ginny—see if you can fix a fire, will you? We've got to boil up some water and—'

'Save yo' strength,' the black man husked. 'You got to get back to yo' brother, girl. Round up them cows an'... an' press on north to Forty Mile. Don't... don't want no invalid slowin' you down.' He forced a grin. 'Jus'... jus' leave my by the side o' the trail an' haul off my boots...'

'Ches,' the girl said firmly, bending over in order to stare directly into his face. 'Listen to me. Forty Mile can wait. We'll get there sooner or later. But right now, let's take care of you.' She pulled out a kerchief and wiped his ebony brow. 'You might be hurting like hell,' she told him bluntly. 'But you're not going to die. Do you hear me? I won't *allow* you to die. So quit feeling sorry for yourself.'

'But I—'

'Chester...'

He nodded weakly. 'Yes'm.'

'Good. Now—about that fire.'

She climbed to her feet, pausing when she found O'Brien watching her appreciatively. Meeting his gaze and forcing a strained smile, she brushed a lock of auburn hair away from her face and said softly, 'Thank you, O'Brien. For... well, for—'

'Forget it,' he replied.

She shook her head. 'I'll *never* forget it,' she said.

And then, in a warm and feminine gesture that was completely at odds with her former arrogance, she came forward and kissed him gently on the cheek, just as the five surviving Tlingets topped the ridge to the north and hurried on down to join them.